JF
DUE

DD Sticker Removed & taped are 6/22/06 ¿m

Emma Eileen Grove

MISSISSIPPI, 1865

———❤———

by Kathleen Duey

———❤———

Aladdin Paperbacks

For Richard
For Ever

First Aladdin Paperbacks edition April 1996
Copyright © 1996 by Kathleen Duey
Aladdin Paperbacks
An imprint of Simon & Schuster
Children's Publishing Division
1230 Avenue of the Americas
New York, NY 10020

Library of Congress Cataloging-in-Publication Data
Duey, Kathleen.
Emma Eileen Grove / Kathleen Duey. — 1st Aladdin
Paperbacks ed.
p. cm. — (American diaries ; #2)
Summary: Twelve-year-old Emma receives unexpected
friendship from a Black roustabout and a Union soldier during
an explosion on the steamboat Sultana in 1865.
ISBN 0-689-80385-0
1. Sultana (Steamboat)—Juvenile fiction. [1. Sultana
(Steamboat)—Fiction. 2. United States—History—Civil War,
1861–1865—Fiction. 3. Shipwrecks—Fiction.] I. Title.
II. Series.
PZ7.D8694Em 1996
[Fic]—dc20 95-26674

Randall has left Claire and me alone—with strict orders to stay in the stateroom. Claire is napping, so I am able to write. I meant to make an entry every evening, but it has been almost ten days since I have written. So much has happened. Lincoln is dead. Some still say it isn't true, but most believe it now. He was shot in a theater. I hated him, but it will go even worse for the Confederacy without him, Randall says.

It has been a weary time since we left home. Flooded roads, absolutely mired in mud, all the way on to Crescent City. Many were traveling, like us or worse. The war is over, but the countryside is ruined, people starving everywhere.

Randall bought us cabin passage on the Sultana, a paddle wheel steamboat. Steamship travel! (Like a proper belle!) And more food than I have seen on a table since Papa enlisted. The river is swift brown water as wide as one can see. Mr. Cass Mason, the captain, says this is quite bad, even for spring. Passed a cow and calf on the bank yesterday, muddy and sad, ribs sticking out.

Saw Vicksburg day before yesterday—the city

is torn up. Houses ruined and holes all over the bluffs from our fortifications and Yankee shells. They loaded paroled Yankee soldiers there—so many that the Sultana tipped far to one side when all of them crowded to the rail for a photographist at Helena this morning. They look so weak and thin from the war prisons they were in. I could feel sorry for them if they were not Yankees. An opera troupe has played twice—they are going to Memphis to perform.

I want to wire Uncle Simeon, but Randall says we should not waste the money. It worries me that he never answered our letters.

Oh! They are singing again. I hate these Yankees.

CHAPTER ONE

Emma paused in her writing and sat up straight. Her hair brushed the underside of the top bunk. Claire was still asleep, her dark hair fanned across the narrow cot. Her somber little face made Emma frown. Claire was seven years old, yet she never sang or laughed. She rarely even smiled anymore. Emma clenched her fists. Damn Yankees.

An uneven chorus of "John Brown's Body" was rising up from the Union soldiers who crowded the main deck. Emma tensed. She was sick of Yankee singing. At least the day before they had mostly sung from the hymn books the

Christian Commission women had handed out. Now they were resorting to war songs.

Emma punched her feather pillow, then patted it smooth as the song spread through the prisoners' ranks to the hurricane deck overhead. She longed for fresh air, but no one could walk the long decks through the throngs of thin, ragged men. They all looked sick, and they were filthy. The song got louder. The Yankees weren't singing so much as shouting now.

"He's gone to be a soldier in THE ARMY OF THE LORD . . ."

Emma put her fingers in her ears, but it did no good. The Yankees were jammed into every corner of the decks and stairwells. Their torn blankets were laid out, inches apart, if they had blankets at all. They had all been in Confederate prisons, held until they could be exchanged for captured Confederate troops. But now the war was over.

The voices out on the decks rose another notch. Emma's stomach tightened. Since dawn she had heard the released soldiers moving around on the tarred and graveled hurricane deck overhead. It sounded as though every one of them was singing as they got to the third verse.

"John Brown's knapsack is strapped upon his

back. HIS SOUL IS MARCHING ON. Glory, Glory Hallelujah. GLORY, GLORY, Hallelujah. GLORY, GLORY HALLELUJAHHHH . . ."

The ceiling creaked, metal on metal. Emma cringed, but she refused to look up. At Vicksburg, the ship's officers had scurried over the *Sultana*, directing the roustabouts and deckhands. They had nailed up extra supports and shoved posts between the hurricane deck above her head and the boiler deck beneath her feet—then between the boiler deck and the main deck below it. Once the work was done, they'd loaded on more of the soldiers. Emma sat still, wishing Randall would come back. She began swinging her feet against the mattress board, concentrating on the soft clunking sound, shutting out the singing, pushing the Yankees from her thoughts.

More than anything, Emma wanted her father. His last letter had come nearly nine months before. Maybe he was still alive somewhere. But if he was, he'd make it home to find no one there. Randall had left messages with neighbors and letters nailed to the door lintel. But what a terrible homecoming for her father! News that his wife was dead and his children had fled north to Uncle Simeon's. Emma banged her feet harder against the cot, then glanced at Claire.

She was still sound asleep.

"They'll hang Jeff Davis from a SOUR APPLE TREE AS THEY GO MAAAAARCHIIIIING OOOOON."

The last verse always made Emma feel sick. Jefferson Davis was still president of the Confederacy. He was a great man who had fought passionately for independence and freedom, and he had remained honorable and a gentleman throughout the war. That was certainly a lot more than the Yankees could say for themselves.

The roaring song faded, and Emma's foot-banging suddenly seemed absurdly loud. She stopped, feeling foolish. Claire stirred on her cot as though the sudden silence had disturbed her more than the noise. She sat up, rubbing her eyes. A light knock on the door made Emma start.

"Ladies? Are you in there?"

Emma recognized the high feminine voice. She went to the door and pulled the handle, opening it a crack, then wider when she saw Mrs. Gibson's plump pink face. Mrs. Gibson had boarded at Baton Rouge and had taken to Claire immediately, charmed by her sweet face and sad eyes. "Hello," Emma said politely. Claire looked startled but not afraid, so Emma added, "Come in." As Mrs. Gibson entered the stateroom, Emma automatically looked at her dress.

Emma's mother's sewing had gotten the family through the first part of the war. After their father had enlisted in the army, she had used her egg money to buy the last four bolts of satin from Jarford's Dry Goods Store. She had made two gowns and sold them both. Once people had seen her work, she'd been hired by wealthy ladies from all over the county. But then, after Confederate money became worthless, even the plantation women had stopped having new dresses made. By the end of the war, the work was all alterations and mending, bartered for cracked corn or a little flour. The war had made everyone poor.

"Emma?" Mrs. Gibson sounded faintly annoyed, and Emma realized she had been staring at the rose pinks embroidered on the hem of the woman's princess dress for too long. She blushed, but Mrs. Gibson smiled. "I wondered if the two of you might like to accompany me into the saloon for a lemonade? I saw Randall go out. He isn't back yet, is he?"

Emma shook her head. "No, but—"

"Then come. It just isn't healthful for children to be cooped inside like stew hens."

"We'd best not. Randall would never forgive me," Emma apologized. "I gave him my word."

Besides, she thought, we only met you a few days ago. She glanced at her sister, hoping she wouldn't start crying. But Claire was calm. She sat attentively, watching.

"Your word?" Mrs. Gibson echoed, her eyes widening theatrically. "To stay in this airless little room all afternoon long?"

"Just until he gets back," Emma defended her brother. "My father charged him with our care in his last letter." She blushed again. Why was she telling Mrs. Gibson that? It was none of her business.

Mrs. Gibson adjusted her skirt. Her daytime costumes were only modestly hooped, a style Emma's mother had approved of; if hoops were to be worn at all, they should not be overdone. Emma felt her eyes sting. She missed her mother so much. She turned her head so Mrs. Gibson wouldn't notice and ask what was the matter.

"Randall has great admirers in his sisters," Mrs. Gibson said brightly. "Little Claire fairly dotes upon him."

Emma pressed her lips together. Since their mother had died, Claire had clung to Randall like a vine to a porch rail. She had stopped asking when their father would come back. He had been gone almost three years, after all. All Claire wanted now was to be with Randall every second of the day.

"Do come," Mrs. Gibson insisted, motioning toward the door. She opened it and stood aside. The saloon was crowded. Emma saw a pretty young woman in a pearl gray silk dress pass by, her posture perfect. Voices rose and fell in aimless chatter. Mrs. Gibson winked and nudged her arm. "Accompany me. Please. We will remain within arm's reach of this very door."

Emma couldn't help but smile a little. Mrs. Gibson was like some of the plantation women who had hired her mother to sew. She was always fanning herself or fiddling with a dainty parasol; her voice was lazy, soft, and musical. She was completely charming. Everything seemed to amuse her. She was smiling now. "Please?"

"As long as we can see him when he comes back," Emma said, talking herself into it.

Mrs. Gibson gathered her skirts, the steel hoops clicking against the wall behind her. Emma scooped up her diary and pushed it beneath her pillow, hoping Mrs. Gibson wouldn't notice. But, of course, she did.

"Ah! A journal. That's a good way to practice seemly composition. Just be careful not to write what should be kept only in your heart."

Emma's hands hovered over the pillow for a moment. She often worried that Randall would read her diary. She had been keeping it ever since she had turned twelve, about six months before, in the leather-bound book her mother had used for sewing accounts.

"I want Randall," Claire said in her unhappy little voice. She was sitting up, dangling her legs over the edge of the bed. Her eyes were round, fixed on Mrs. Gibson. Claire was small for seven, and it seemed as if during the past year she had gotten younger, not older. She still cried for their mother when her nightmares woke her—until she remembered that Mama had died of the fever.

"Come on, come on," Mrs. Gibson urged. "Randall will be back shortly. Would you like lemonade?" Claire nodded.

Emma took Claire's hand and led her to the door. Mrs. Gibson ushered them through it, moving with graceful charm, like a lady bringing guests into her own grand parlor. Emma felt Claire tighten her grip at the sight of all the people.

The usual crowd of men stood at the dark oiled-wood bar or sat at the small tables clustered in front of it. The row of chandeliers sparkled and swung gently with the motion of the steamship.

Waiters were setting up the long portable table in preparation for supper. Emma pulled her sister closer, resting her free hand on Claire's shoulder as they walked on the thick carpet.

"It is just too crowded with all these soldiers," Mrs. Gibson was saying. She patted her gold necklace. "So many *Yankees*. I do hope your valuables are somewhere safe?"

Emma was silent. Randall thought everyone they met was out to steal their remaining money and their mother's gold wedding band. She involuntarily touched the waist of her dress where she had sewn the ring into the seam. She could not possibly lose it. Randall carried their last two gold coins stitched into his trouser cuff.

"Yankees, Em," Claire breathed. "Look."

Emma watched two Federal officers stride into the long, narrow saloon through the ornate forward doors. Their uniforms were faded but clean. They looked freshly shaved, bathed—not ragged and sick like the men on the decks. So they had not been in Cahaba or Andersonville prison like the others. But like all Yankees, they seemed to move too quickly and their voices were too loud.

"Come on," Mrs. Gibson said in a high singsong voice, as though she were cajoling babies.

"Don't stare. Come on, come on."

Emma tried not to feel annoyed—Mrs. Gibson was a nice woman. She was on her way home to St. Louis, returning from a visit to her family's plantation near Baton Rouge; she had lived in St. Louis since her marriage ten years before. She was rich. She said she hated Yankees, but she had never missed a meal or spent a night shivering, hiding in a thorn thicket. No one had ever stolen her blankets or emptied her henhouse. Emma was sure Mrs. Gibson had never wished for griddle cakes until her stomach cramped at the thought of warm food.

Mrs. Gibson guided them past the polished bar where men stood smoking cigars and drinking whiskey, past the dark-suited gamblers and well-dressed traveling businessmen. On the far end of the long narrow room, near the doors that led to the more sedate ladies' cabin, she found an empty table and sat them both down. Then she perched on the edge of her chair, her skirt hoops tilting dangerously upward as she got settled. After a moment of smiling vaguely at nothing at all, she clapped her hands lightly to catch the attention of the Negro waiter.

"In one moment, Ma'am," he said politely, turning to go back into the kitchen.

"At home," Mrs. Gibson began without prompting, "we'd do our needlework on the lawn. The house servants would bring lemonade or sometimes mint tea. We'd sit and just talk and sew. The breeze would come over the levee and you could hear the darkies working in the fields singing so beautifully. The most lovely old hymns . . ." Her voice trailed off so gradually that Emma wasn't sure whether Mrs. Gibson had stopped midsentence or if she had just whispered the end of it. She sighed prettily and was about to begin again when the Yankee officers appeared at the table next to them.

Mrs. Gibson looked up impatiently as they pulled back their chairs and seated themselves. One was quite a bit older than the other, Emma noticed. He had gray in his beard.

"Makes no sense to anyone," the younger officer was saying. "I can't think why they didn't put some of them on the *Lady Gay*. Does Captain Mason have a deal with Hatch?"

The older officer shook his head. "How could I know? There's good profit in carrying them, that's certain. Five dollars a man."

The younger man whistled softly. "That much? There must be two thousand of them."

Emma watched the two men out of the

corner of her eye. She hadn't thought about how much money the *Sultana* must be making with this many passengers on board. As she listened, the officers changed subjects.

The older man shrugged. "R. G. Taylor made a boiler patch in Vicksburg, so I was told. He argued that it needed more than that, to be safe. Left the boat, but they talked him back to do it."

"R. G. Taylor worries too much," the younger officer said, laughing. "Mason's the smart one. I'd have put on another two hundred soldiers for the money."

The older officer grinned. "Where? In the kitchen?" He stroked his beard. "They wouldn't care. They just want to get home."

The younger one grimaced. "They look like death, don't they? The Secesh prisons were hellish, to hear them tell it." Emma stared into the men's faces as they talked. What would she do if she ever saw the Yankee who had taken her mother's blankets? She exhaled slowly. She never would. It didn't matter. She hated them all for it.

"I want Randall," Claire whispered.

Emma bent close to her ear. "He'll be back quick as anything. Don't you fret."

"At last," Mrs. Gibson sighed as the waiter approached them, then smiled graciously as she asked for three lemonades. She patted her hair and touched one finger to her cheek. "A little extra sugar? Please?" Emma tried not to laugh. Mrs. Gibson was at least forty, and she giggled and simpered like a girl of sixteen.

Claire was looking at the opposite end of the saloon, the ceiling, the door that led into the ladies' cabin—anywhere but at the Yankee officers next to them.

"Is your home close to Baton Rouge?" Emma asked, to start Mrs. Gibson talking again. Claire had enjoyed listening to her stories the day before. Maybe more stories would keep Claire from fidgeting and watching for Randall.

Mrs. Gibson preened, obviously flattered by Emma's interest. "Well, yes, Peachtree is not too far from Baton Rouge. We passed it, coming north on the river." She paused to smooth her short, fitted Spenser jacket, then smiled wistfully. "The big house is just below the levee. We used to listen for the paddle wheelers, then we'd run out onto the veranda. It was wonderful to look up the hill and see them glide past. When the river was flooded far enough up the levee, the pilothouses would be higher than the yard trees." Her eyes went soft, focused on her memories, not the saloon bustling with cabin passengers.

The Yankee officers were talking again, and Emma felt Claire tensing. "You said yesterday that you had dances there?" she urged Mrs. Gibson.

Mrs. Gibson smiled. "We had summer dances with paper lanterns on the grass. And croquet games. My eldest brother was quite wicked at croquet." She touched her perfect hair, her cheek, then her bodice in quick, nervous movements. Emma looked enviously at Mrs. Gibson's waterfall hairdo, a cascade of thick sausage curls. Were they real? If not, the horsehair fall had been dyed perfectly.

"At twenty I married Mr. Gibson and moved to St. Louis." Mrs. Gibson's eyes flooded with tears, which she quickly wiped away. "It's all gone now, anyway. Peachtree, I mean. Everything's changed." She glanced at the Yankee officers, then away. She leaned forward and whispered. "They will reinstate slavery, you know. They will. When they realize that cotton and tobacco can't be grown without field labor." She looked sidelong at the Yankees. They were absorbed in their own talk, not paying any attention to her at all. She raised her voice a little. "They didn't care about the darkies. Their mill workers are less well off than most slaves, not knowing where their next meal will come from. No. They just wanted *control* over us."

Emma didn't answer. She had heard a dozen explanations for the war; everyone had an opinion. She didn't know, and the truth was, right now she didn't care. All she wanted was to get safely to St. Louis and to find Uncle Simeon. She squeezed Claire's hand, then tried to let it go. Claire held on. Emma wiggled her fingers to keep them from going to sleep in Claire's grasp. At least she wasn't crying. Emma saw the woman in the pearl gray silk again. She was beautiful, her long brown hair braided and crimped, her skin like milk.

Emma shifted awkwardly in her seat. Who would have ever imagined that she would be sitting in a steamboat saloon with people like this? Her father wasn't exactly a peckerwood—he could read and he was a gunsmith—but he had never owned even one slave. Their farm lay in a valley, cramped between two huge cotton plantations.

Emma touched the snow-white tablecloth with one finger. All her life she had seen the carriages pass, filled with merry young people on their way to places she could only imagine. It would be so strange to have servants who did all the chores, to wear stiff crinolines, French perfumes, and gowns that took hours and hours to press. Or to be sent to some female academy instead of learning her letters reading her father's yellowing books by firelight.

Emma sighed, watching a regal older woman in a green satin dress with wide sleeves inset with lace strike up a conversation with Mr. Gambrel, the ship's clerk. She looked down at her own faded cotton dress. She would never belong in a place like this.

Mrs. Gibson was sitting perfectly straight, gazing brightly at nothing in particular. Claire's hand tightened on hers as the Yankee officers' voices rose again.

"It was the rifles that made the difference," the older man was insisting. "If they could have got more Henrys, we'd have been in for it. Their Enfields were good enough until the repeaters came through. Thank God they never had enough of them."

His companion nodded. "My boys started out with a higgledy-piggledy mix-up of Belgians and muskets and even a few old Halls—every smooth-bore squirrel gun anybody's father could spare. The Enfield is a good weapon. But I'm with you. If the Henry repeaters had come up sooner, the war wouldn't have lasted a year." He set down his glass with a sharp little rap to punctuate his words.

Emma saw a look of sorrow cross the older

Yankee's face. "Both sides, so many dead. And the cotton states ruined for a generation at least. It's a tragedy beyond any other." He took a pipe out of his breast pocket and tapped it on the edge of the table.

Emma stared at him. He looked sincere; his regret seemed real. Why? His side had won. Randall said that all the Yankees wanted was to make the Confederate states crawl.

"Ah!" Mrs. Gibson cried out in delight as the waiter carried a tray toward them. He lifted tall lemonade glasses from the tray to the table. He set a dish of sugar and a long silver spoon next to her. "Oh, you dear heart," she said warmly, smiling.

Emma watched the waiter's face. He was smiling, but it seemed strained. Maybe he had been a plantation house slave, and Mrs. Gibson's cordiality only reminded him of it. She would have to ask Randall about the Negroes on the *Sultana*. She had noticed that none of them ever went ashore at any of the landings. Maybe they were freedmen from up north somewhere and afraid to get off. No Negro could walk the streets without risking confrontation. They could be jailed as runaways or beaten up for claiming to be free. People were terrified of a slave uprising now.

Mrs. Gibson gave the waiter another dazzling smile, then dismissed him with a flick of her graceful fingers. She turned to Claire. "You are going to like this, aren't you? I surely hope you will, Honey."

Claire didn't answer, but she reluctantly let go of Emma's hand long enough to lift her glass, lean forward to drink, then set the glass down. An instant later her hand sought Emma's again. "I want Randall," she said quietly.

"Of course you do," Mrs. Gibson soothed. "Whatever is he about?" She arched her brows at Emma.

Emma was about to answer when a commotion at the far side of the room caught her attention. The bright skirts and dark suits parted amid gasps and practiced little feminine screams. A very tall, very thin man was standing in the forward doorway carrying a boy who had blood smeared across his face.

Emma scraped back her chair and found herself standing. She hurried across the room, pulling Claire as she went, staring at the unconscious boy whose feet dangled, swinging against the tall man's leg. It was Randall.

CHAPTER TWO

"I reckon he'll be fine," the tall man was telling Mr. Cross, the steward, who stood with his hands on his hips. More and more of the passengers were noticing, their conversations stilling.

Emma dodged around Mr. Cross, dragging Claire, whose grip on her hand had tightened painfully.

"You his kin?" the tall man asked.

Emma stared at him, then at Randall's white face. She nodded, working Claire's fingers loose so she could touch Randall's cheek lightly. Claire started to cry, holding Emma even tighter.

"He got to insulting some of the boys," the tall man said, and Emma dragged her eyes from Randall back to his face. He was one of the prisoners. A Yankee. His cheeks were gaunt with starvation, and an unhealthy odor still clung to him. Emma wrinkled her nose, struggling to free herself from Claire's clutching hands. She had to get Randall away from this Yankee, get him back to their stateroom.

"I can carry him wherever you want him set down," the tall man said. He was looking earnestly into her eyes. "I don't think he's much hurt, miss. Just maybe his wind knocked out and his nose bloodied."

Emma gave up fighting Claire and picked her up. She was heavy, too big to be carried like a baby, but she instantly calmed down, burying her face in Emma's hair.

"This is disturbing the other passengers," the steward said sternly.

The Yankee frowned. "Ah, well, hellfire, Mr. Cross, I could hardly leave him laying out on the—"

"His cabin," the steward interrupted firmly, "is this way."

The tall man looked down at Emma and

tilted his head. "Can you walk with that load?" He jutted his chin at Claire.

Claire nuzzled her face into Emma's neck. Emma held the Yankee's gaze and nodded. "She's afraid of you."

The tall man looked uncomfortable. "Well, I'm sure 'pologetic, Miss. I reckon I look pretty sorry all right."

"Come along now," the steward urged them. He turned to lead the way.

The tall man shifted Randall higher in his arms and swung past Emma, making his way through the crowded saloon behind the steward. The bartenders paused in their work; talk buzzed a little louder at every table they passed. Emma felt like screaming at them all to mind their own business.

At the cabin door, with its oil painting of a beautiful mountain scene, Mrs. Gibson was standing, fanning her pink face with one hand. Emma patted Claire's back automatically when she whimpered. Mrs. Gibson, with a little flourish of her skirts, turned to pull the handle downward and pushed the door open just as they got close. The Yankee led the way in, hesitating until Emma managed to get around him and nod at Claire's cot. "There."

The Yankee laid Randall down awkwardly. Randall rolled onto his side. His eyelids raised enough to show the shine of his eyes, then lowered. He groaned, but his breathing settled into a steady, deep rhythm.

"See?" the Yankee smiled. "He'll be fit in no time. He just needs to work a little bit on his manners."

Mr. Cross still stood in the doorway. He cleared his throat. "This area is reserved for the cabin passengers," he said in an even voice.

The Yankee looked up. "Surely, Sir. Of course it is." His voice was polite, but Emma saw a flash of anger in his eyes. "You serve in the army, Sir?" he asked the steward. "Federal or Confederate?"

Mr. Cross didn't change his expression. "I am to see that the cabin passengers are comfortable."

The Yankee glanced around the cabin, and for a second, Emma saw his eyes light. She followed his glance. A tin of crackers lay open on the foot of the upper bunk where Randall had slept. Was he that hungry? Emma wondered. Probably. The Yankees had obviously not been well fed in prison. But they had destroyed the farms they'd passed all over the South, especially General Sherman. Emma shivered with hatred. People said Sherman's army had killed and burned *everything*.

"Please, Sir," Mr. Cross prompted.

The Yankee touched his forehead in salute in the general direction of the steward. Then he ducked through the doorway and was gone. The steward looked from Randall to Emma, then back. Emma turned, whispering in Claire's ear. "You have to walk, Claire. I can't carry you any more. You're all grown up and heavy." Reluctantly, Claire slid down from Emma's hip to stand beside her, but she held fast to Emma's left hand.

"Thank you kindly," Emma heard Mrs. Gibson say. "I will stay to assist."

Her words seemed to free Mr. Cross from his uneasy stance just inside the door. "Call upon me if you need anything," he said formally, bowing a little from the waist toward Mrs. Gibson. He looked grateful to be dismissed. Mrs. Gibson fluttered a hand at him and he went out. She closed the door behind him.

Emma sat next to Claire on the lower bunk. "You have to let me take care of Randall." She tried to keep her voice calm, even though she was frightened. What if Randall was really hurt? What would they do?

Claire raised her head. Her face was very pale. "He hurt Randall. He stinks."

Emma smoothed her sister's hair back.

Claire even sounded like a baby lately. Emma glanced at Mrs. Gibson, who nodded reassuringly. "Just sit here and watch," Emma told Claire. "I'm not going anywhere except to wash Randall's face." Claire only held her hand tighter. Emma took a breath. It was so hard to stay patient with Claire. Randall was much better at it than she was. He could always talk her into doing what was needed.

"I will sit with Claire," Mrs. Gibson began.

"No, thank you," Emma said quickly, knowing that Mrs. Gibson's attentions might only make Claire worse. "If you would wet the towels?" Mrs. Gibson crossed busily to the washstand. The pitcher was almost full. "Please, Claire," Emma pleaded in a whisper. "I have to go *now*."

Claire released her hand. Randall moaned a little louder, and Emma picked up her skirts and turned before Claire could grab her hand again.

"Here." Mrs. Gibson was holding out the wrung towel. Emma took it and sat beside Randall. She touched the cool cloth to his face and he flinched. Carefully, she wiped at the blood that masked his cheeks and chin. It was quickly apparent that the Yankee had been right. Someone had hit Randall hard enough to give him a nosebleed and knock him senseless for a few minutes, but there were no cuts or bruises anywhere else on his head or face. His breathing was normal, too.

Randall opened his eyes for a second, then closed them again. "Em?"

"I'm here, Randall." She sat back, resting her hand lightly on his forearm. She heard Claire make a frightened little sound, but she refused to turn and look at her. If she did, Claire would come scuttling across the room to Randall.

"Em?" His eyes were still closed.

"Yes. I'm here."

"I gave them one or two for Ma's quilts. Remember that day?"

Emma could only nod. She would never forget. On that chilly morning, the hoofbeats had rung out against the bluff above the house. She had gone to the little window. Her stomach had clenched when she saw the blue coats and caps. Yankees. She had never seen Federal soldiers before, but she had heard how cruel they were. Everyone knew the stories.

Shaking with fear, she had waited. When they pounded upon the door, Randall had flung it open, his father's musket at his shoulder. Before he could fire, the soldiers had knocked him aside and taken the gun. Emma had watched helplessly as her mother had gotten up from her sick bed and, following first one blue-coated soldier then another, begged them to spare enough to keep her family alive. They had ignored her. Finally, her shrill voice had been stilled by a fit of coughing. Worn out and defeated, she had had to return to bed—a bed now without linens or a quilt.

The officer in charge was as ragged as the youngest private. Randall had argued with him, explaining that they owned no slaves, that his father thought slavery was wrong. The officer had finally ordered Randall taken to the smoke shed. They had thrust him inside and dropped the lock bar.

"If you come out, rebel cub, we'll shoot," the officer had said, his teeth glinting in a quick smile. Emma had been terrified then. Randall had a hot temper. For a long time she could hear him beating at the door, but it was heavy oak.

Laughing and boasting, the soldiers had loaded their saddlebags with all of the meat and sweet potatoes in the root cellar and all of the milk and butter from the springhouse. Some of them had looked ashamed, but they went about their thieving anyway, avoiding Emma's eyes, walking quickly past her mother's bed.

"I gave them more than two," Randall said

clearly, his voice breaking into Emma's memories. A smile touched his mouth and wrinkled his nose. He flinched again, opening his eyes. "I gave one of them a bloody mouth." He reached up and carefully felt his nose. "Lord, this hurts."

Mrs. Gibson bent over the cot. Randall looked confused for a second, and Emma realized he hadn't known she was there. Mrs. Gibson smiled brightly. "You seem to be feeling somewhat better." She clicked her tongue. "You should know that you gave your poor little sisters a terrible fright."

Randall sighed. He met Emma's eyes for an instant, a fierce, quick glance. Then he closed his eyes and spoke faintly. "I think I should rest now."

Emma took her cue and faced Mrs. Gibson. "Thank you ever so much for your help. Perhaps we can take supper together, once Randall has rested."

Mrs. Gibson made a polite little sound and reached out to pat Emma's cheek. "I would enjoy that so very much," she said cordially. "It is just so very oppressive with all these Yankee prisoners aboard. One can barely stand it. We can be grateful that Captain Mason says they are only going as far as Cairo."

Emma waited a moment, then took a step

toward the door, remembering how her mother had always gotten rid of Mrs. Simmer, the neighborhood gossip. "I am sorry you could not stay longer this time," she said evenly, avoiding Randall's eyes, which had reopened into two glistening slits. His mouth was twitching at the corners. She knew if she looked at him they would both start laughing.

Mrs. Gibson gathered her hooped skirts and swayed around the end of Claire's cot, reaching out to pat her cheek. Claire allowed the touch, which surprised Emma.

"A little later, then," Mrs. Gibson said. "It is time for my nap, but I will look for you at supper."

Emma smiled. "We'll see you then. Thank you again." She opened the door. When Mrs. Gibson had rustled her hoops and petticoats out, she shut it and leaned against it.

Randall sat up slowly and Claire leaped to her feet. She flung herself at him, almost knocking him down again. "Claire," he said, his voice tight. "You are hurting me."

Claire released him, then carefully settled herself against his side. He repositioned himself, grunting and wincing, then put one arm around her shoulders. Claire, Emma thought, was the one person in the world who had nothing to fear from Randall's temper. For her, he had almost endless patience.

"Why is she mother-henning you two so close?" Randall demanded, poking one finger at the door Mrs. Gibson had just passed through.

Emma shook her head. "I'm not sure. I think she's just lonely. Maybe most of the others don't want to hear her talk about her daddy's plantation all the time."

"She's rich?"

Emma nodded. "Or was. Her father has a big place somewhere around Baton Rouge. Raised cotton and tobacco, I guess, before the war. I can't remember everything she's said. She talks all the time. She's nice enough, and she lives in St. Louis."

"Well, I guess she's harmless." He stroked Claire's hair.

"Did you find out when we dock in Memphis?" Emma kept her voice casual. She was hoping desperately that they could wire Uncle Simeon before they got to St. Louis. Farther south, the telegraph lines were either war-ruined or humming endlessly with Federal army messages and the news of Lincoln's death. Now, Randall argued, it would be throwing money away—they'd be in St. Louis in a week.

Randall touched his nose carefully. "I talked to Mr. William Snow, a senator-elect from Arkansas." He paused for his grand announcement to have an effect on her. Emma obliged him by widening her eyes. "Oh, yes," Randall said proudly. "I talked to him in the saloon before I went out on deck. He said he'd spoken to one of the pilots and that we'd be getting into Memphis by early evening."

Emma smiled at her brother. He was so excited about having talked to an important politician that he had forgotten all about his nose and the Yankees. He was studying her face. "I don't want to spend the money to wire now, Em."

"Oh." Emma could feel Claire watching her. She tried to conceal her worry. "Well, it's all right, though, isn't it? Just because Uncle Simeon doesn't know we are coming doesn't mean he won't be happy when we get there. Does it?" She smiled and knew Claire could see she was pretending. She kept the smile on anyway. It was better than letting Claire see how afraid she was.

They hadn't had a letter from Uncle Simeon in nearly two years, even though they had written him three times. Had something happened to him? What if he wouldn't take them in? What if he *couldn't*?

CHAPTER THREE

"Maybe we should have stayed home," Emma whispered to Randall. They had climbed to the upper bunk. Claire was lying on her own cot, absorbed in her dolly.

Emma sat cross-legged on the end of the upper bunk, as Randall turned and propped himself up on one elbow, finding a tolerable position for his bruises. "Em, that's crazy talk. How could we? There was no seed to plant, and no one who had any was selling it. And how could we have done it without the mules? I couldn't pull the plow. Maybe we could together, but who'd guide it down the furrows? Claire?"

Emma frowned at him, but Claire didn't look up; she either hadn't heard her name or she was ignoring it.

"I just mean he might not even be there," Emma whispered after a moment. "He never answered our letters. For all you know he was killed in the war. Maybe he fought for the Federals."

Randall sat up. "Uncle Simeon is not a Yankee. Never. He would be as against Lincoln trying to ram orders down our throats as Pa was."

"He's lived away from Louisiana for a long time, Randall. And he never owned slaves."

Randall looked past her, over her head, and she could tell his patience was wearing thin. "Slavery," he said slowly, "is an evil thing, but it did not cause the war. Slavery is already dying. You know what Pa said. Killing half the men in the country isn't going to help even one Negro learn to read or learn a trade to take care of himself. Pa was right."

"A lot of people think different," Emma argued. "Mrs. Gibson said the Emancipation Proclamation will be revoked. Her mother's house servants wept when they heard they were free."

Randall shook his head. "Then they were old

and it just scared them, that's all." Randall pinched the bridge of his nose. "It's starting to ache pretty fair. He really laid me down, that Yankee. Well, he was only about ten feet tall. I guess I picked a good one to call a yellow-backed coffee-boiler."

"Tall?" Emma's eyes flickered toward the door. It hadn't occurred to her that the man who had carried Randall in had been the one to hit him. What had he said? She tried to remember and couldn't.

Randall didn't seem to notice her confusion. "I hit him twice. But it was like trying to fight a stilt-bird. He probably *did* hang behind his regiment to boil coffee so he could get captured. Coward."

Emma remembered the man's face. She hoped that Randall wouldn't. "It's best if you stay out of fights."

Randall shrugged. "I just get to thinking about Ma. How can you forget, Em?"

"I'll never forget," she shot back at him, angry at the suggestion. "You're the one who wants to go live among Yankees, not me."

Randall sat up straight. A thin trickle of blood started from his nose, and he reached for the towel. "I'm just trying to take care of you and

Claire," he said, dabbing at his face. "Pa wrote that letter. He will expect you safe and sound when he finds us." He stood up, trying to pretend nothing hurt. "I want to go back out on the deck. I can't stand being shut in here. I start to feel sick."

"Me, too," Claire piped up.

"I don't like it, either," Emma admitted.

"It isn't proper for the two of you to be out among all those prisoners, though. Em, they're *Yankees*."

"I want to go out, I want to go out, I want to go out," Claire began to chant. This had been her favorite way to get Ma to give in when she was three or four years old. She danced on one foot, stretching up, her hands just reaching the lower edge of Randall's bunk. "I want to go out, I want to go out."

Randall slid down and hugged her. "Then we'll go."

A knocking sound above their heads made them all stop talking and look up. The pounding went on for half a minute, then ended abruptly. Randall wrinkled his brow. "Maybe some prisoner was tapping out his pipe. Or getting the sand out of his boots."

"Half of them don't have shoes," Emma said,

still staring at the ceiling. It was strange to think of the hundreds of ragged men on the deck above them. It made the little stateroom seem even smaller and stuffier. Claire began her chant again. Randall took her hand. "Leave Dolly here, so you don't lose her."

Claire looked up at him, her eyes full of adoration. She ran to put Dolly in her cot, then skipped back. Emma found herself watching them. It was as though Claire had taken all the love she'd felt for her parents and fastened it onto her brother. Emma sighed. The war had changed everything. "Are you sure you're all right, Randall?"

Randall answered by crossing the room, Claire at his heels, clutching his hand. He opened the door and made a little bow, like a grand butler at a ballroom. Claire laughed. Randall held his pose. "Hurry up, Em. This hurts."

She went out, then paused. The saloon was even more crowded now. The tables near the bar were all full. Emma self-consciously hurried to keep up with Randall.

"They have an alligator somewhere," Randall said over his shoulder with exaggerated casualness.

Emma stopped in her tracks. "A what?"

Randall grinned. "An alligator. The *Sultana* crew keeps it as a mascot."

Emma shook her head, disbelieving. Randall widened his eyes and arched his brows to make fun of her expression. "Yes, they do, little sister. I heard some of the Yankees talking about it."

Claire pulled at Randall's hand. "An alligator?"

Randall smiled down at her. "Maybe we could go see it."

Emma shook her head. "I don't think we should leave the saloon. The Yankees . . ."

"Stay, then," Randall said quickly. "But we paid our fares. If I want to go somewhere on this steamboat, there's no Yankee going to keep me from it. I won't find another fight," he added, looking at her intently. "Not if you and Claire are with me."

Emma smiled uncertainly.

"Claire? Do you want to see the alligator?" Randall asked. She nodded, quick little jerks. "See?" Randall said to Emma. She smiled again, giving in.

Randall led the way through the dapper traveling men. There were only a few women passengers, and most had probably returned to their cabins to rest before dressing for supper.

Normally, many of the cabin passengers would have been out on the decks, watching the forests and farms go by. It had rained off and on all day, but it wasn't the weather keeping people inside:It was the Yankees piled onto the *Sultana* like cordwood.

Once they were out on the deck, it was hard for Emma to keep up with Randall. He had picked Claire up and was weaving his way through the crowds of soldiers. Most were sitting up, talking, but many were napping, curled up like huge, emaciated children. Some had the sunken eyes of men who were about to die. At the head of the stairway leading down to the main deck, Randall hesitated, waiting for Emma.

"Miss? Miss?" Emma refused to look for the owner of the voice. She kept her eyes on Randall and made her way toward him, hoping he would not hear. As much as she hated Yankees, she did not want Randall fighting anymore—and he might, no matter what he had promised.

If Randall had gone to be a soldier, he would never have survived the war, of that she was sure. His very nature would have prevented it. She was grateful that he had been a little too young and saddled with the responsibility of taking care of her and Claire. It had saved his life. The day the

Yankees had locked him in the smokehouse, she had waited until the last of them had ridden out of sight before letting Randall out. She had opened the door to find him standing ready with a haunch of meat for a club. If she had been a Yankee, he'd have smashed her skull. And gotten killed for it, almost certainly.

"Miss?"

This time, startled out of her thoughts, Emma turned before she could catch herself. She found herself looking up into the earnest blue eyes of the Yankee who had carried Randall into the saloon. He was smiling now. "I'm sorry. I got four sisters, one of 'em about your age."

Emma had no idea how to respond. He doffed his cap respectfully and looked into her eyes. "Your brother is all vinegar, miss. I know he's bitter. I am. All of us," and he gestured to include his comrades, "got about as much reason to curse rebels as anyone. This war has wore everybody right down to their souls." He looked past her. "I'm pleased he's only got a sore nose."

Emma could see in the daylight what she hadn't seen in the dim saloon. The Yankee was not just thin. His bones shoved at his skin. His gums were red and swollen, and he had sores on his scalp and his hands. He noticed her looking and replaced his hat, then pushed his hands into the pockets of his ragged pants. The patches on his thighs were wearing thin and tearing loose. The holes at his knees were so big there was barely enough cloth to suspend the frayed cuffs at his ankles.

"I miss my sisters, real sharp," he said. "I considered them a plague before the war, I admit."

"Emma!" It was Randall. He was glaring at her over Claire's head.

The Yankee glanced up. Without another word he moved aside and she almost ran, intercepting Randall. She caught at his arm. "Randall? Randall. I want to see the alligator, that's all. I was asking him if he knew where it was." She glanced back. The Yankee had sat down and was talking to someone. Without his height to give him away, maybe Randall wouldn't recognize him.

Randall tilted his head, shifting Claire's weight from one side to the other. Emma, having lied, had no idea what to say next. Randall was studying her face. She took in a big breath and looked up at the fancy fretwork bordering the top of the deck. "He said we had to go that way," she said vaguely, waving her right hand in an equally imprecise gesture that took in half the *Sultana*.

Randall didn't bother to answer. He frowned, then started off again, walking a little more slowly and looking behind more often. Emma, aware that many of them were staring at her, was careful not to make eye contact with any of the men they passed. Their attention made her angry. If they missed their sisters and wives and daughters so much, why had they started the war to begin with? They should have let the Confederacy separate from the United States instead of following the tyrant Lincoln into battle. All the South had ever wanted was to make its own decisions. Why couldn't Yankees understand that?

Randall paused between the tall wheel-houses, the plank structures that enclosed the huge paddle wheels. Here, close to the smoke stacks, the hiss of steam and the metallic pounding of the pistons were uncomfortably loud. Randall glanced at Emma, then hailed a mustached man lounging near the boiler room doors. The man took his pipe from between his teeth and leaned forward to listen as Randall shouted near his ear. His coat was a fine pinstripe, and he had a gold chain showing from his pocket.

"With all this weight," the man shouted back, gesturing widely enough to take in the soldiers packed on every deck, "they are hard put just to keep up the pressure. I can't let you down there now. Too dangerous, Son."

Through a narrow doorway, Emma could just see the stokers, their skin shining with sweat, orange-brown in the hot light of the coal fires they were tending. The black chunks of fuel seemed to fly from their shovels, arcing out in an even rain upon the glowing coals in the fireboxes. Gauges and valves were everywhere.

Randall was still talking to the man, shifting Claire so he could see around her. She was pressed against his chest now, her feet dangling on either side. Randall was probably asking questions about the engines. He was fascinated with such things. Emma strained to hear but couldn't. The pounding of the boiler engines was relentless. She moved closer.

"Randall?" Claire said loudly. The din erased the rest of what she said, but what she wanted was obvious. She began tugging at Randall's collar. She put her forehead against his cheek and spoke right in his ear, leaning back and forth, trying to force him to walk away from the heat and noise. The mustached man tried to pat Claire's head. She shrieked and began to cry. Grim-faced, Randall shouted a question. Emma heard the word *alligator*.

The man smiled at Randall, then at Emma as she drew nearer. "They got tired of everyone taunting the poor creature," he yelled, loudly enough for her to hear, too. "These soldiers are like men back from the grave. Like children. Anything delights them." Then he leaned close to Randall again and said something more, gesturing.

"They put the alligator in a closet under the stairs today, to keep him from harm," Randall said to Emma, his breath tickling her ear. Randall led her around a corner. The metallic pulse of the boilers softened a little, and Emma was grateful. They were behind one of the wheelhouses, she realized. She could hear the blades, shaped like huge troughs, slapping against the water.

Randall stopped. There, set into the wheelhouse wall, was a door, standing open. Inside was a huge wooden crate, its white-oak planks scarred and scraped as though it had been dragged from one end of the *Sultana* to the other.

A bearded man in rough trousers and a homespun shirt was approaching them. Randall asked him if they could see the alligator. He grinned. "Right there. I kin lift the cover for you." He stepped around and gripped the edge of the thick planked lid. For a moment or two he strained at it; then he glanced around and roared, tipping his head back. "Hosiah? Hosiah, git yerself over here!"

A Negro roustabout came around the corner. He went to the far end of the crate. Between the two burly men, the lid slid easily back. Hosiah leaned to look in, his face fearful. "Scares me. Always did."

Emma stared at him. Whether or not he had been a freedman before the war, he was free now. Or would Congress revoke the Emancipation Proclamation as Mrs. Gibson believed?

Hosiah met her eyes and she looked aside, confused by a sudden feeling of shame. Would he hate her if he knew that her father had fought for the South? If the Confederacy had won, there would be no question at all about Hosiah's remaining a slave.

Randall stepped forward with Claire and stood on tiptoe to look into the crate. "He's big," Claire said admiringly. Randall hooted with laughter and winked at the bearded man.

"Want me to lif' you up, miss?" Hosiah held out his arms to Emma. His hands were huge. His arm muscles bulged from the heavy work he did day in and day out. Emma glanced at Randall.

"Sure. Sure she would," he said, grinning.

"Just be careful, Em. Don't lean in too far." He laughed again.

Emma reluctantly approached. Hosiah drew a circle in the air with one finger, and she turned to face the crate. She felt his hands on her waist. A second later she was looking down at an alligator so big it was hard to believe it was real. It raised its head and snapped. Its eyes were dull. It writhed in a quick circle and clawed a little way up the side to snap blindly again. Emma jerked back involuntarily. Her heart ached for the alligator. What a horrible life, shut in a dark box, with the maddening pounding of the steam engines ringing endlessly through the wooden crate.

Hosiah held her steady a minute longer, then set her down so carefully that she didn't bobble or lose her balance at all. She turned to thank him and found him looking back over the edge of the crate.

"I wish," he said, glancing down at her, "they would jus' let the poor ol' man go back to his swamp."

"It's cruel," Emma said.

"This world is sure enough a cruel place, Miss," he agreed, touching his forehead in farewell. Then he turned and disappeared. Emma stared after him.

CHAPTER FOUR

Tense and uncomfortable, Emma followed Randall and Claire down the stairway to the main deck. On every step two or three Yankees sat side by side looking out over the river or talking. So many of them had only one arm or one leg or foot—amputations performed by army surgeons who could not repair limbs shattered by artillery shells. Emma thought about her father again and felt goose bumps rise on her skin. So much had been lost. What had been gained?

The main deck was even more crowded than the boiler deck. In addition to the soldiers, there were the regular deck passengers—white people who couldn't afford cabin fare, and the Negro passengers. This was where the *Sultana*'s crew slept, too. Emma recognized one of the cooks. Some of the deckhands and roustabouts lounged against the rail, unneeded or taking a break from their labors. Emma saw several women off to one side. Wives? Or maybe they worked on the *Sultana*, too. She had seen a few women cleaning rooms and passing in and out of the kitchen.

"Emma?"

She hurried to catch up with Randall. She was glad he had impulsively bought them cabin passage, even though it had taken almost half their money. She couldn't imagine trying to sleep on the bare planks of the main deck, surrounded by so many strangers and the throngs of skeletal Yankees.

"Keep closer," he chided her when she got to him. "Stop staring at people. I just want to go the stern for a few minutes, then we're going back up. It's almost suppertime."

As they made their way aft, Emma heard the pens of squealing hogs that crowded the stern. There were horses and mules, too, tethered in long lines. They stood as if stunned, confused by the water rushing beneath them.

Finally, Randall found an area somewhat less crowded, on one side of the stern rail. The river was so wide. To the east, on the Tennessee shore, the late afternoon sunlight fell on clumps of bushes, seemingly growing right out of the dark water. Emma was puzzled, then figured it out. The river had risen far enough to cover the trees on the flood plain. The "bushes" were really the tops of tall trees.

Emma leaned against the rail and faced the water. She let out a long breath, then inhaled. The air was clean and fresh. For a few moments she could pretend that the deck behind her was empty, not filled with the crowds of Yankees. She watched the water, the currents wrestling with each other beneath its muddy surface.

The Arkansas shore was so far away that Emma couldn't see it, only a line of low hills somewhere beyond that met the gray sky to form the horizon.

"Suppertime," someone sang out.

Emma watched three or four Yankees carry buckets down the stairs. From nowhere, tin plates began to appear in almost every hand. Emma saw one man unroll his blanket to reveal a plate wrapped inside. Another pulled his from inside his shirt.

"Let's go. Keep closer this time," Randall said, gripping her shoulder. Without another word he started back through the crowd. Emma tried to walk as fast, but it was hard. The men were passing the buckets of hardtack bread among themselves along with hunks of dark meat. It looked raw and she shuddered. She could see some of the sweet crackers the Christian Commission women had handed out the day before, rolled up in scraps of cloth and saved like the dainties of a tea party. The Yankees were laughing and talking, seemingly as happy with their crude supper as if it were a feast.

A swell of shouting made Emma stop and look up. The Yankees were gesturing, pointing out at the river. There, coming toward them, was another paddle wheeler. It was much like the *Sultana*, shining white and shaped like an elongated three-tier wedding cake.

"Too bad it ain't going our way," one of the Yankees lamented. "We could have had a race."

"With this many aboard? As skinny as we are, we weigh the *Sultana* down considerable." Laughter broke out, then traveled toward the bow as the joke was repeated.

The steamboat approached quickly, making much better time downstream than the *Sultana* was making against the current. Its hurricane deck, and the little square cabin built on top of it, were trimmed in bright green. On top of that perched the glassed-in pilothouse, just like the *Sultana*'s.

"I got to go up in the pilothouse yesterday," Randall boasted, leaning toward her. "Had to go through the texas to get there." Emma wrinkled her forehead. Randall shrugged as if astounded by her ignorance. "That little cabin beneath the pilothouse. It's the officers' quarters, but they call it the texas."

Emma looked back at the approaching paddle wheeler. On her hurricane deck, dozens of people stood at the rail. Women with bright parasols and fluttering skirts began waving. Delighted, the Yankees hooted and whooped, waving back.

"They call it that because one paddle wheeler named every stateroom for a state, but then Texas came into the Union and they wanted to honor it, too. So they called the officers' quarters the texas—and the name spread up and down the river." Randall smiled suddenly, and Emma could see how proud he was to have been in the pilothouse, talking to the *Sultana*'s crew. For an instant she envied him fiercely. He could go anywhere he wanted to, and no one thought it was improper.

"Want to see the pilothouse before supper? I think there's time. Maybe we could get someone to take us up there."

Emma nodded, her envy warming into excitement. Randall set Claire down and led her through the throngs of high-spirited soldiers. Emma hurried to keep up. Randall went straight back along the main deck, sticking to the lower level this time. As they walked, Emma felt the men watching her as they would watch an unfamiliar bird flitting past. She found herself looking into one face, then another, wondering if they had families. Did their families know they were still alive? Did her own father look like this now? Ragged and bony and dirty from some Yankee prison? Her heart ached. They wouldn't dare, would they? The Confederate soldiers had only defended their rights and their homes. An image came into her mind of her mother, flushed with fever, arguing with the Yankees. The memory was so strong that it slowed her, dragging at her spirit.

A sudden cheer from the Yankees made her turn around. The other steamboat was passing the *Sultana*. She tooted her whistle. The *Sultana* blasted a response. The soldiers cheered, waving and yelling greetings at the passengers on the other boat as they passed. JENNY LIND was painted in flourishing script across her wheelhouse. The sun was low on the horizon. The brown water seemed gilded, reflecting its light. The cheer fell to silence and the men were quiet, watching the *Jenny Lind* fall quickly astern.

Randall was frowning. Claire wriggled in his arms, her face petulant. "I don't want to go to the pilothouse. I'm hungry," she blurted out. "I want roast chicken." Her voice was loud, and it seemed to touch each hollow face, every pale cheek around them. Every man who had heard was looking at her. Claire's face went pink with embarrassment. She hid against Randall's shoulder. Emma wanted to yell at the Yankees, to tell them that they had gone without decent food for months, too. Claire was not a spoiled little girl, she was a starving one—still thinking every rich meal aboard the *Sultana* would be her last. The Yankees stared and Emma glared back at them, defiantly.

"Come on, Em," Randall muttered. He was disentangling Claire's arms from about his neck, making her slide down, setting her back on her feet. Claire, gripping Randall's right hand with both her own, glanced nervously around at the Yankees. Randall started off again, pulling her along, making his way between the bedrolls and the circles of men who had looked up from their supper of hardtack and cold meat.

Claire began to whimper. Randall picked her up again, turning to make sure that Emma was still close behind. Then he hurried up the stairway, past more Yankees who moved politely to one side. Once they were back on the boiler deck, Randall walked a little faster, carrying Claire through the last of the ragged war prisoners. Only when they were inside the saloon doors did he finally pause.

The hushed, deep-carpeted room was like another world. There were the perpetual drinkers and card players, but many others had joined the crowd. Some of the traveling men had female companions. The six or eight other women passengers were in the saloon now, too. As they had every other night, the women had changed their day costumes for fancier, brighter evening wear.

The waiters were setting up for the meal, laying silver and placing glasses on the long table. Emma followed Randall to the far side of the saloon. They slid into chairs at one of the smaller tables. Claire, her face still tense and unhappy, plopped down beside Emma. She stared back toward the ornate forward door they had just come in. "I want them to go away."

"I know," Emma answered, understanding her. "I do, too."

"Most of them are getting off at Cairo," Randall said, pulling back a chair for himself. "They'll put them on trains there, ship 'em home."

Emma heard his voice catch. She saw a little shadow leap across his eyes. Home. So her fearless brother was homesick, too. It made her feel better, not worse.

"What do you think it'll be like?" she ventured. "In St. Louis."

Randall's eyes had hardened again and he shrugged. "I expect Uncle Simeon will get us into schools. He's like Pa that way. Book learning will be part of it, at least for me. I'll work, too. I'll earn our keep somehow."

"I can sew," Emma said. "Not like Mama did, but I can mend and alter pretty well. I could take in laundry, too. And people say girls and women are working in the mills."

"I don't want you working in a mill. Who said it?"

Emma tried to recall. So much had happened in the past few weeks. Suddenly she remembered. "A lady waiting for her husband. While you were asking fares in Crescent City and Claire and I stayed on the dock."

Randall didn't answer. His mind was already elsewhere, she could tell. As long as whoever had put the idea in her mind wasn't around to continue the bad influence, he wasn't interested. Randall waved at a waiter. Emma envied him again. If something wasn't immediate or important, he dismissed it. Her own thoughts tended to pick at things, to dwell on them far too long. Claire was like her, too; she was pretty sure. Like their mother. Their mother had always done the worrying.

Emma looked around the saloon. The chandeliers were sparkling overhead. So many faces, Emma thought—more strangers than in her whole life. And she would be unlikely to ever see any of them again. Or to recognize them if she did.

No, she thought, correcting herself. *I would know Mrs. Gibson, certainly—and the tall Yankee, and the Negro Hosiah. And maybe the man with the mustache.* She tried to picture his face and couldn't. But she would know Captain Mason, she was pretty sure. He was handsome. She blushed at the thought.

"Em!"

"Yes?"

"Maybe we should just go take our places. Other people are starting to."

Emma looked. The long table was slowly filling. "Mrs. Gibson," she said, remembering. "I told her we'd take supper with her."

Randall frowned. "I wish you hadn't."

"I'm hungry," Claire whined.

Emma was hungry, too. Her mouth watered as she thought about the meal they had eaten the night before. There was so much food aboard the *Sultana*—at home they had often dreamed about having enough meat again or butter or enough flour for biscuits. The *Sultana* seemed to have everything.

They went and sat at the long table. The waiter poured their glasses full of water. "The meal tonight is roast chicken, sweet potatoes, corn mush, and biscuits."

"Biscuits," Claire echoed in her whispery voice. "And gravy?"

The waiter bent forward almost imperceptibly, tilting his head. "I will not forget that gravy." He walked back toward the kitchens. When the door swung open, Emma could see the enormous wood stove, its silvery shelves clean and shining, the big iron kettles spouting steam.

Randall sat back in his chair. "I want to live like this forever. Food when you ask, everybody polite and nice. They treat us like rich folks."

Emma nodded. They had eaten poke weed at home. Weeds! She never wanted to be that hungry again in her whole life. Randall clasped his hands behind his head, looking around. "Maybe I can start a business someday, a dry goods, or be a banker like Uncle Simeon."

Emma closed her eyes, imagining it. Living in town would be strange at first, but she was pretty sure she would like it. The worry that Uncle Simeon might not help them crouched at the edge of her thoughts, but for once, it didn't leap out to kill her hope. She pictured herself walking down a boardwalk, her dress flounced and full in back, a black velvet paletot coat fitted over it.

"Hellooo," a familiar voice rang out.

Randall frowned. "Hasn't she got anything to do but pester us?" he asked between his teeth.

Claire was twisting around in her seat to see Mrs. Gibson approaching. "Claire likes her," Emma chided Randall quietly. "And we told her we'd eat with her."

"*You* did," Randall whispered.

Emma shrugged and leaned forward to whisper back. "She tells her plantation stories. It's like princess tales to Claire."

"I hope I am not disturbing you all," Mrs. Gibson said as she got close.

Randall just sat for a second. Emma glared at him. He got quickly to his feet. "Ma'am."

Emma smiled up at Mrs. Gibson, imitating the smile her mother had used for guests. "Please do join us." She paused when Mrs. Gibson looked from her to Randall, then back again. "You have met my brother, Randall?" she asked, taking the hint.

"Not entirely properly," Mrs. Gibson said, and spread her hand lightly across the base of her throat. "I am very pleased to make your acquaintance. Your sisters are charming, and they have spoken of you in the most glowing terms."

Randall managed some polite-sounding mumble. He arched his eyebrows at Emma while Mrs. Gibson turned to Claire. "Your brother seems quite recovered. Isn't that wonderful?"

Claire nodded. "He called them Yankee cowards." She pulled in a breath and lifted her chin. "We saw an alligator in a box."

Emma blinked. Claire hadn't strung that many words together in months. Randall looked incredulous. *See?* Emma mouthed silently when he met her eyes, tipping her head to indicate Mrs. Gibson. Randall nodded reluctantly.

"Perhaps," Mrs. Gibson said in her velvet voice, turning to face Randall, "you would be kind enough to help me with my chair?"

Randall stepped back so quickly that his own chair almost tipped over. He caught it and set it straight. Mrs. Gibson sidled back, and waited while Randall pulled her chair out. Then she lowered herself carefully onto the very edge of the chair seat, pulling her skirt hoops gracefully into position. Emma watched, fascinated, as Mrs. Gibson settled herself. Her mother had never worn hoops, though she had sewn dozens of hooped party gowns and daytime costumes for her clients. She had always said only wealthy women could wear them, women who didn't have to turn a hand at work.

"It has been an exciting afternoon, I gather," Mrs. Gibson was saying. She was addressing Randall. He nodded and looked around uneasily. "I have just been so homesick all morning," Mrs. Gibson added, then paused again.

Claire tilted her head like a little bird. "Why?"

Emma looked at her sister as Mrs. Gibson reached over to pat Claire's hand. Claire let her do it for a moment, then pulled her hand slowly back. She kept her eyes on Mrs. Gibson, though, expectant. "Why?" she repeated. "Why are you homesick?"

"I hadn't seen Baton Rouge in nearly five years until last week," Mrs. Gibson began. She sipped water from her glass, then set it down with a little sigh. "Well, of course I walked about, taking it all in. I went up Laurel Street, all the way to Church Street. All the shops, and the Veranda House and Rosenfield's Dry Goods . . . everything seemed so strange and so familiar at the same time. There's a man there, a Mr. Lytle, who makes good portraits. I thought about it, as a memento. Then I left. Who wants a portrait of me?" She turned her head slightly.

"I would," Claire said quickly.

Randall had been looking around the room. Now he set his elbows on the table and focused on Mrs. Gibson. His face was lit as though he had just had an idea. "Where is your husband?"

Mrs. Gibson sat back as though someone had struck her. "That is an impertinent question, young man, which you have no right to ask."

Emma heard the little sound of dismay from Claire and turned to see her looking back and forth between Randall and Mrs. Gibson. She probably hadn't understood what had been said, but she could feel the tension.

"I didn't mean anything by it," Randall defended himself, looking half angry. "I just wondered."

Mrs. Gibson was recovering, fanning at the air with one hand. "I'm sure you did not mean to offend, Randall. There is no mystery. I am a widow. My husband died less than a year ago." She sighed. "I apologize for my rudeness. I am absolutely not myself presently."

Across the saloon the woman who had worn the pearl gray silk sauntered along near the stateroom doors. She was in sky blue now, with wide epaulets of dark ribbon and flounces at her hem. A man with a huge black beard hailed her. Emma tried to watch without seeming to stare. The man was from the Chicago Opera Troupe. He had played banjo and sung at the performances they'd staged for the Yankees.

"Wouldn't it be a terrible life?" Mrs. Gibson asked knowingly. "No home. No family."

Emma tried to imagine the lives the musicians led. There were women who performed and sang—though not nearly as many as there were men. Some people thought it very improper for any woman to be on a stage for any reason, even singing hymns and patriotic songs. Claire has a lovely voice, Emma thought suddenly. That was one more thing the Yankees had taken—Claire's happy nonsense songs.

"Memphis," a ship's officer called from the forward door. "Memphis in about twenty minutes. Dock time approximately three hours. If you leave, be sure to return before departure."

Emma heard the Yankees on deck echoing the news, shouting it out so quickly that there would be no need for a second announcement anywhere aboard the *Sultana*.

Mrs. Gibson stood. "Let's go see if we can see the rooftops, Claire. You can just begin to spot them now. The late sun glints off the windows, sparkling like fiery little stars." Randall frowned. Mrs. Gibson waved away his concern with an airy gesture. "We will go only to the end of the saloon, not more than twenty feet out on the deck. We'll be back before supper is served. Will you come, Claire?"

Claire hesitated, leaning involuntarily toward Randall. Then, abruptly, she pushed back her chair. "Yes," she said. Astonished, Emma watched Mrs. Gibson's lead Claire away. Head high, curls bouncing, Claire looked almost like the little girl she had been before the war had taken everything away.

"I can hardly believe it," Randall whispered.

In a few moments, Mrs. Gibson and Claire were back and the waiters were bringing tray after tray of steaming plates. The fragrance of roast chicken filled the long saloon, and Emma reached beneath the table to pinch her own leg. She wasn't dreaming.

CHAPTER FIVE

Mrs. Gibson talked throughout the meal, first about her mother's chicken receipts, then about a cook named Auntie Ruth who had made delicacies envied by every neighboring plantation family. Claire was rapt, pushing her gravy back and forth with her spoon, her eyes glued to Mrs. Gibson's face.

Mrs. Gibson touched her hair at her temples, smiling. "Oh, I do enjoy your company, Claire. You look so like my daughter . . ." She trailed off, her charming smile straining at the corners of her mouth. Emma sat still, unsure what to say. Randall was looking off across the saloon. He might not even have heard. If he had, he was acting like he hadn't.

"Where is she?" Claire asked. "Does she have a dolly?"

Mrs. Gibson pulled a handkerchief from the bosom of her dress and dabbed at her eyes. She looked so distraught that Emma frowned at Claire. "Don't ask people personal questions, Claire. It's rude."

"No, no, it's not her fault," Mrs. Gibson said quickly. "My daughter died of smallpox. I just miss her." Her eyes were shining with tears.

Randall stood up, awkwardly facing Mrs. Gibson. "Excuse me, please. I'm going to make my way down to the bow. If some of the Yankees are getting off, I'd like to be at the head of the line."

Emma shook her head. "Randall, don't go."

He scowled at her. "Why not? I want to see Memphis."

Emma lowered her eyes. Before she could speak, Mrs. Gibson leaned toward Claire. "Would you care to play a game of checkers in the ladies' cabin?" She looked up at Randall, then Emma. "Half an hour or so? I will bring her to the stateroom for an early bedtime."

Randall cleared his throat impatiently. "That'd be fine." He looked at Emma. "I'll be back soon. Don't worry about everything so much."

Mrs. Gibson stood, beaming, then led Claire past the bar and opened the door of the ladies' cabin. Claire stopped and waved at them, but then she followed Mrs. Gibson through the door. Randall looked at Emma. He gestured toward their stateroom door. "Go on now, Emma."

Emma pushed her chair back and stood up, straightening her skirt. She didn't say a word. Randall was fidgeting, excited, and probably didn't even notice that she was upset. But she was. He ordered her around too much.

The saloon, dim in spite of the crystal chandeliers, smelled of cigar smoke, whiskey, and the elaborate dinner that had just been eaten. Emma longed to go out on deck where the sun was low to the west and the evening breeze was fresh. Instead, she opened the stateroom door and went in without looking back. She slammed the door behind her, then flopped down on Claire's cot and stared at the ceiling.

The metallic creaking overhead began almost immediately. Scuffling noises followed.

Emma narrowed her eyes and shook her fist at the invisible Yankees, hating them. She sat up and lit the little oil lamp they'd brought from home—it would cast less light than the wall lamp, but she could set it close on her bunk. Then she pulled her diary from beneath the pillow. She read her last entry, then got her pen and ink bottle from her bags.

Randall has left again, this time to go walk about in Memphis while we are docked here. He can go wherever he wants, it seems. Claire is off playing checkers in the ladies' cabin with Mrs. Gibson, a woman from St. Louis who is traveling on the Sultana. *Claire seems more her old self with Mrs. Gibson. I am sitting in our stateroom, waiting for them to return.*

The scuffling on the hurricane deck began again and Emma flinched, trying not to look up, trying to ignore the noise.

I will be so relieved when these Yankees are let off in Cairo. They have made our river trip into a nightmare. Randall got into a fight with one of them and was carried back. I hope that he doesn't get into more trouble while he is ashore in Memphis. He got into fights at home sometimes, but it did not scare me like

*this. I suppose it is because Claire and I
depend on him so. What would I do if
something happened to him, if he were hurt?*

*Randall says he thinks Uncle Simeon will
make us go to school. I would be glad of that.
There are female academies in St. Louis, I
think. Perhaps I will be able to go to one. It
seems like a dream, that something good could
come from so much sorrow. Most likely I will
work at mending and laundering. I wonder
what mother would have thought of that? I
think that she would want me to go to school
if I could, or to marry well enough that I could
raise my children and care for my home
without taking in extra work. Yet, she was
happy. I know she was, and that she loved
Father and was content with her life. Oh,
God, where is my father?*

Emma set down her pen, her eyes flooded
with tears. She really was frightened about Uncle
Simeon's, about going to St. Louis. Randall
wasn't—or at least he wouldn't talk to her about
it if he was. She closed her eyes and lay down,
tired.

A soft knocking at the door brought her out
of her doze. "Emma? May we come in?" It was
Mrs. Gibson.

Emma stood quickly and slid her diary back under her pillow. She replaced her pen and ink; then she opened the door. Claire was leading Mrs. Gibson now.

"I won!"

Mrs. Gibson nodded, maneuvering her wide crinoline-puffed skirt through the narrow door. "She did. I shall have to practice." She yawned and covered her mouth delicately. "I beg your pardon," she excused herself. "I am fatigued this evening." Emma nodded politely, wishing Mrs. Gibson and Claire had played checkers a little longer. It had been weeks since she had been alone for more than a few minutes, and she had spent it napping.

"Good-night, Claire," Mrs. Gibson said, smiling. She looked at Emma. "Claire says that your Uncle Simeon has not written you?"

Emma nodded slowly. Why would Claire have told Mrs. Gibson that? Had Mrs. Gibson been asking questions?

"I would hope that if anything goes awry . . . I mean, if he cannot . . ." She trailed off and touched her lips with one graceful finger. "I am a widow, Emma. My daughter died and . . . I am alone. The company of a little girl . . ." She trailed off again. "Well. Perhaps it is foolish to speak of it now." She looked down at Claire. "I will see you in the morning," she said, her face lit with a smile. Claire smiled back.

"Look," Claire said, the moment that Mrs. Gibson had left. She held up a length of deep blue ribbon. "Mrs. Gibson gave it to me."

Emma made a fuss over the ribbon, but her thoughts were elsewhere. Mrs. Gibson hadn't been very clear, but Emma was uneasy about what she'd said—or what she *hadn't* said. Was she talking about taking Claire away from them? Emma wanted to tell Randall about it. But, of course, he probably wouldn't be back for a few hours.

"Time for bed, Claire," she said, when she realized that she had been silent too long.

Thumping overhead startled them both. "Damn Yankees," Claire said.

"Claire!" Emma was shocked. "You shouldn't use language like that."

Claire looked defiant. "Mrs. Gibson says they are damned. So do you and Randall."

Emma didn't know what to say. She pulled Claire's dress off over her head. "Go wash." Claire went to the washstand. "Use soap," Emma reminded her.

Emma shivered, wishing that she still had

the blue flannelette nightgown her mother had made for her, but the Yankees had taken it along with everything else. It had probably been cut to pieces, stuffed down Yankee boots for extra warmth. The thought made her ill.

Someone on the hurricane deck above began singing.

"*All quiet along the Potomac, they say . . .*" Emma was startled to hear the familiar words and sweet, mournful tune coming from Yankees. Everyone knew it at home. It told a terrible, sad story of a homesick sentry getting shot—it always made Emma feel like crying. The song quickly spread from one deck to the next, from bow to stern. As the tragedy unfolded from verse to verse, Emma saw Claire's little frown reset itself upon her lips.

Emma clenched her fists. What was wrong with these Yankees? Did they have to remind everyone of every terrible thing that the war had caused? Couldn't Claire have one happy evening? Finally the long song ended and the men fell silent.

"Emma?" Claire's voice was very small. "I want Randall."

"He's ashore, but he will be back soon," Emma reassured her. "Here's Dolly."

Claire took the rag doll their mother had made for her and waited as Emma turned down the cot. She climbed in and burrowed into the pillow. Emma watched Claire close her eyes, wishing she could fall asleep, too. Claire looked so peaceful—maybe her nightmares wouldn't wake her tonight.

Emma sat on the lower bunk, listening to Claire's breathing become slow and even. The scraping sounds overhead had stopped. Maybe the Yankees had settled in for the night, too. Emma found herself looking up one wall, then across the ceiling, and down the other side. The stateroom was so small.

Impulsively, Emma stood and crossed to the door. It wasn't likely that Claire would wake up in the next few minutes. Emma eased the door open, glancing back to make sure Claire was still asleep. Then she went out and closed the door carefully behind her. She would be gone three or four minutes, no more than that, she promised herself.

The deck lamps were already burning, smoking in the chilly breeze. Emma stood close to the saloon doors, shivering, letting the clean fresh air brush against her face.

Here and there a few men sat in circles, talking or companionably silent, but most were lying down now. Emma could actually see most of the way along the deck—though in the lantern light, a lot of detail was lost. She narrowed her eyes and pretended that the Yankees weren't there, that the *Sultana* was carrying her to safety and that everything was going to be all right. Then, feeling a little better, she turned back toward the stateroom.

CHAPTER SIX

Emma woke to a crashing roar that seemed to consume the world and everything in it. Her whole body curled up, trying to escape the incredible, painful concussion that slammed at her ears. She heard Claire cry out, then a booming echo rolling back to the *Sultana* from some distant bluff. Only then was she sure she wasn't dreaming. She struggled to sit up.

Claire was sitting rigidly on her cot. Emma heard high, panicked shouts and screams in the saloon. Scrapes and thuds beat upon the hurricane deck above their heads.

"What is it?" Claire was screaming. "Randall, what is it? What is it?"

Emma stood up. Her knees were weak, shaky. Claire, her eyes wide, was as pale as milk in the dim light. Emma looked to the top bunk. Randall was not there. For a moment, Emma was confused. Then she remembered. Randall had gone ashore and she had finally gone to bed, too tired to wait any longer for him.

A strange squealing began directly overhead, metal scraping against metal. Another deafening crash wrenched through the *Sultana*. Claire put her hands over her ears, whimpering in fear. The sound freed something in Emma. They had to get up; they had to do *something*.

As Emma reached for her clothes, she felt a strange vibration in the floor. Still clumsy from sleep, she pulled her dress on over her nightgown. "Claire!" Emma shouted close to her sister's ear.

"What's happened?" Claire shrieked back at her. "What's wrong?" Her voice was rough, scraping its way across Emma's pounding ears and frightened heart. There was only one explanation. Emma knew it, but she did not want to say the awful words aloud. She looked at the top bunk again. Where was Randall? Where *was* he?

Emma managed to get Claire's dress over her head, but then Claire flailed and turned, crying for Randall. Emma grabbed at her. "Claire! Let me get you dressed. Then we can go out." Fighting like a frightened animal, Claire wrenched around. Emma managed to get Claire's arms in the sleeves, then jerked the dress down into place. Breathing hard, Emma picked Claire up and sat her on the cot and got her shoes on, tying them crookedly. Her hands were trembling. Emma scooped up her own shoes, then stepped past her sister and put her hand on the door lever.

When she pulled the door open, she gasped. A thick fog filled the saloon, burning her eyes and lungs. Steam, Emma realized. Steam mixed with smoke. So it was true. The boilers had exploded. And the smoke meant that the *Sultana* was on fire. Cries and groans came through the choking mist. The chandeliers, still lit, swung back and forth, forming soft globes of light sailing eerily in the mist. The stacks of bottles behind the bar had fallen, a mad jumble of glass and spilled liquor.

Someone screamed close by. Emma gripped Claire's shoulder and bent to speak into her ear. "If the boat is sinking, we have to get off. There's only one lifeboat, and the Yankees on the stern will have it by now. We have to swim to the dock." Claire nodded. Another, smaller, explosion rumbled beneath their feet.

Emma's thoughts spun. Were they still at the

Memphis dock? They had to be. Randall wasn't back yet. "The life belts," she said, amazed that she was only now thinking of them. She went back in and dropped to her knees to pull the cork belts from beneath the bunks. Her hands were shaking so badly that she could barely fasten the buckles across her own chest. Claire stood still this time, so still that Emma had to push her to the door once her belt was on.

"I want Randall," Claire said in a whisper.

"We'll find him," Emma said, hurrying her out the door.

They entered a sea of voices as they came out of their stateroom and turned toward the forward doors. Emma heard a man scream and a woman shouting hoarsely. They sounded close, but she couldn't see anything through the stinging fog. She swallowed hard, grasping Claire's hand tightly. The air was so hot, so smoky, that every breath was painful. Emma blinked, trying to see. Instinctively, she covered her mouth and nose with one hand, but it did no good. She took tiny, quick breaths, conscious of her hammering heart.

All around them, half-dressed people with wild eyes darted one way or another in the eerie reddish light. Abruptly, Emma realized she had set her shoes down to put on the life belts and had forgotten to pick them up again. She hesitated. She would not need them for swimming, she told herself. The crazed screaming of metal against metal began again over their heads. Emma stiffened. There was no going back now.

They made their way along the saloon wall, avoiding the piles of debris where it had collapsed. Emma saw the bearded banjo player working his way along the opposite wall, a sobbing woman beside him. The pretty woman he had hailed at supper? They seemed dreamlike, appearing out of the smoke, then gone. A Negro man with a woman and child came toward Emma and Claire. Emma turned to see them heading for the door that led to the ladies' cabin. Maybe it would be smarter to go that way—maybe the stern was safer. That was where the little lifeboat was, hanging from its cables. But a lot of people would be trying to use it, Emma was sure. They'd have no chance of even getting close. And the bow was closest to the dock. Emma hesitated, then led Claire onward.

"Fire!" a man shouted, plunging through the forward door to the saloon. "Buckets! We need buckets!" He ran to rummage through the contents of the bar, then darted through the smoke into the kitchen. Emma could hear the sound of dishes shattering.

"There's hundreds scalded to death," the man screamed when someone shouted at him for dumping the cupboards onto the floor. "Buckets, fool! Do you want to burn?"

Emma couldn't hear an answer, but the man ran back out of the saloon, passing them a second time. He carried a flour tin in one hand and a cheese box in the other.

"How far are we north of Memphis?" a man asked, appearing out of the fog. He looked into Emma's face and his eyes clouded. "You're a child! God help us!" He staggered past, hanging for a second onto Emma's arm, then vanishing into the smoke again. A few seconds later, Emma could hear him asking the question of someone else.

"Where's Randall?" Claire whined. Emma pushed her along without answering. Above Memphis, the man had said. So they weren't still at the dock? Emma felt a chill crawl across the back of her neck. Where was Randall? How long had she been asleep?

They were almost to the forward door. Emma felt a quick pain in her right foot. Broken glass was scattered all over the floor. As she lifted her foot to pull out the shard of glass, a voice separated itself from the din of panic that surrounded them. "Leave him. Leave him here. He's dead. Can't you see that!"

"I won't," argued a second voice. "He stayed by me at Antietam. He carried me."

"His legs are broken. He can't swim even if you get him to the water! We are miles from anything by now." The argument went on, but Emma could no longer make out their words. Miles from anything? A piercing fear went through Emma's heart.

"Help me. Please help me."

This was a feminine voice, from behind them in the saloon. It was high and frightened, but Emma recognized it instantly. So did Claire.

"Mrs. Gibson," Claire yelled, whirling around. "Where are you?" Claire held back, twisting, trying to free her hand from Emma's grasp. "Mrs. Gibson?" she screamed.

"Claire?" Mrs. Gibson's voice was louder now. "Emma?"

Claire was hysterical. Calling Mrs. Gibson's name, she wrenched free. Emma could only run after her, back into the smoke, her lungs aching in the acrid air.

"Mrs. Gibson?" Claire screamed.

"Here," Mrs. Gibson called. "Here!"

Emma made her way across the saloon blindly. She had lost sight of Claire and was following Mrs. Gibson's voice. The saloon seemed too wide, the wall too far away, but Emma finally reached the far side and saw them.

"She's stuck," Claire wailed over her shoulder. She was kneeling. Emma got close enough to see. Mrs. Gibson was still on her cot. The stateroom wall had collapsed over her. The wood lay in splintered layers across her blanket.

"Help me," Emma shouted at Claire. "Lift that end."

The chandeliers were still swinging in slow circles. Their hazy shadows lengthened and shortened dizzyingly. Emma and Claire raised the first board slowly. Claire's end slipped but didn't fall. "That way," Emma instructed, nodding to her left. They dropped the board to one side. Then they raised another, heavier one, with shattered planks nailed to one side. Mrs. Gibson rolled onto her side, sliding down to sit on the floor. Claire embraced her. Emma patted Mrs. Gibson's back, unsure what else to do. Dark stains on Mrs. Gibson's nightgown frightened her. Then Emma realized that the stains were her own blood. She had somehow cut her right hand.

Emma tore a strip from Mrs. Gibson's bed

linen and wrapped the cut tightly. Claire had flung her arms around Mrs. Gibson's neck and was crying hard. Mrs. Gibson's hair hung loose down her back. For a second Emma stared at her, stunned. Freed from the intricate hairpins, Mrs. Gibson's hair reached down to her waist. Emma felt herself blush. She had never even seen her own mother like this, in a nightgown with her hair loose.

"My dresses," Mrs. Gibson was saying as she got to her feet, pulling Claire with her. She leaned down to pull on a pair of house slippers, then straightened again. "My dresses are in my trunks. My crinolines are—"

The awful squealing began again, and the ceiling slumped, falling about a foot lower in the center. Mrs. Gibson was standing still, her head tipped back, staring foolishly upward. Emma took her hand, and Mrs. Gibson lowered her eyes. "We have to get out now," Emma said as calmly as she could. She took Claire's hand and gripped it hard.

The ceiling settled again with another shriek of metal. Mrs. Gibson began to cry, but she also began to walk when Emma pulled her forward. With Claire between them, they made their way through the fallen walls and broken glassware to the forward door.

Slanting from its hinges now, the ornate door was on fire. A cinder had caught in the decorative cutwork; the varnish was burning like oil. Emma led Claire and Mrs. Gibson through, and onto the deck.

For a few seconds the three of them stood still, pulling in deep breaths. Out here, the steam had dissipated into the night sky. A breeze pushed slim fingers of fresh air through a billowing spire of smoke that rose from the middle of the *Sultana*. Where it thinned, Emma could see bright orange flames flickering. Beyond it, she could see only darkness.

"We left Memphis," she said, more to herself than to Mrs. Gibson, but Mrs. Gibson answered her.

"Quite late. It woke me around midnight."

Emma coughed, trying to clear her lungs, trying to think. She had fallen asleep waiting for Randall to get back. It was possible that he had returned, then gone out again—that he'd been walking the decks when the explosion came. She shuddered, refusing to believe it. "Randall was late getting back. He must have been. So they left him in Memphis."

Mrs. Gibson was staring at her. "I wasn't going to ask where he was. I thought . . . I thought . . ." Emma nodded. Mrs. Gibson stopped trying to explain.

The smoke shifted, and Emma could see a monstrous X shape, like two fallen giants lying at impossible angles across the misshapen decks. The smokestacks had crashed, crushing the wooden structures between them. The pilothouse was gone, and most of the texas, where the officers had slept. Emma stared. Were they all dead then? And the Yankees who had been sleeping on the texas roof and on the decks?

Mrs. Gibson was shivering violently, her arms crossed over her chest. At least her nightgown had a modest, high collar, Emma thought. She looked away before Mrs. Gibson could notice that she had been staring.

A long scream startled them all. Claire whirled around. Emma held her tightly. A man, his clothing on fire, crawled out of the wreckage in front of them. He stood, then ran, plunging past them toward the stairway, but the stairway was gone. Where the saloon and staterooms hadn't held it up, the hurricane deck had collapsed onto the boiler deck.

Emma stepped away from the saloon door. The little snake of fire had crawled a few feet farther up the wood fancywork. She faced the bow again, her hair blowing back from her face. Fire twinkled through the smoke here and there. The wreckage was quickly catching fire. The wind would bring it this way, wouldn't it? The fire was snapping where the oily varnish was thickest—small, hissing explosions of fresh flame.

Emma's whole body ached with fear. She wished fiercely that Randall were there, that he would just appear—sooty and bruised perhaps, but not hurt—and tell her what to do. Tears flooded her eyes. Emma felt time sliding past, seconds ticking once, then gone forever. The wind lifted Emma's hair. It was getting stronger. Mrs. Gibson and Claire were holding hands, both crying, waiting for Emma to decide what they should do. She took a deep breath, then another, trying to think.

The fire would sweep this way. Jumping into the dark river was certain death if they were miles from shore. Their only chance was to get around the fires, to make their way to the bow.

Trembling, Emma led Claire and Mrs. Gibson into the nightmare of splintered wood and twisted metal, straight toward the screams and the spreading fires.

CHAPTER SEVEN

Jagged edges gouged at Emma's bare feet and she wished over and over that she had brought her shoes. Mrs. Gibson began to pray aloud, bravely at first, but then her voice fell to an uneven whisper as they made their way along the tilted decks. She did not complain, but her steps were mincing and timid even though her house slippers saved her from the worst of the sharp debris. Claire seemed shocked into silence. She hadn't spoken since she had answered Mrs. Gibson's screams.

Many had been hurt in the explosion; many

were trapped in the wreckage. Emma began to feel as though she were floating through a horrifying dream, one from which she couldn't wake up, no matter how scared she got.

Along the last shattered remains of the hurricane deck, above the jagged funnel's edge, Emma stopped, raising her free hand to shield her face against the hot glare of the growing fire. Claire leaned against her; Emma could feel her shivering.

The central portion of the *Sultana* had been gutted. A mountain of lumber and metal had been flung into the air, then had fallen again. Now it surrounded an enormous hole amidships, like a footprint the explosion had left behind. On either side stood the wheelhouses, their inside walls full of holes from the explosion. The huge paddle wheels were still now. Angled between, crisscrossing the abyss, were the fallen smokestacks.

"We can't go any farther this way," Mrs. Gibson said quietly. Her face was beaded with sweat. "It is not possible."

Emma squeezed her stinging eyes shut, hard, then opened them. The sparkles of fire were sparse to the left. There was a dark strip parallel to the rail that looked like it ran all the way to the bow. All along the rail, dark figures were spilling over the side—men jumping to escape the fire. The river all around the *Sultana* would be full of Yankees, hundreds of them, fighting for their lives. "We should wait as long as we can before we jump," she said, thinking aloud.

Mrs. Gibson covered her face with her hands. "I cannot swim."

Claire put her arms around her waist. "I can. I'm a good swimmer. So's Em. You can use our belts."

Emma bit at her lip, angry at herself for scaring Mrs. Gibson—now she was crying again. Claire's pale face was stained by the fire's glow. Mrs. Gibson was turned so that half her face was lit poisonous orange, the other half in ink black shadow. Emma knew her own face was equally grotesque. This is what demons in hell look like, she thought.

Emma led the way again, down the ridge of broken lumber and metal, skirting the edge of the abyss to get past the wheelhouse. Many of the boards beneath them were tarred and graveled, Emma noticed as they descended—part of the hurricane deck. Tar, she thought suddenly, would burn even hotter than varnish. Hotter and faster. As she turned her head, her hair flared out from her cheek. The wind was picking up. It wouldn't be long before the small fires all around them became a solid sheet of flame.

A soft moan, so close that it sounded as though someone were standing beside her, made Emma falter. She spotted two men only a few feet away, hidden by black shadows cast by a section of deck that jutted upward, standing almost vertically. One man was lying down. Emma saw the other bend over, his thin frame doubled up to lean close to his friend. As she watched, he straightened and shook a fist at the sky. It was his moan she had heard, Emma realized. Grief, not pain. His friend had died.

"Emma!" Mrs. Gibson was nudging her.

Emma looked at the Yankee for a second longer. As he turned to face her, a shock of recognition went through her body. The tall man nodded politely, as though they were at a picnic. Emma nodded back. For a moment, she couldn't make herself go on. Mrs. Gibson was staring into the dark sky, her eyes blank. Then Claire tugged at Emma's hand. Emma glanced back toward the cabin that housed the saloon. It was on fire now, and the flames around them were spreading fast, flowing across the wreckage. There was no going back.

Shaking, Emma led the way up a tilted section of the boiler deck, strewn with rubble from above. They had to walk so close to the edge of the fire that her skin prickled with heat. She turned her face away, walking sideways, plucking the thin cloth of her dress away from her skin when it got hot enough to burn.

The wheelhouse narrowed the deck, pushing them even closer to the fire. As they made their way past, Emma pressed against the plank wall, pulling Claire along. Mrs. Gibson's eyes were still empty, her face a mask of terror, but she kept up, holding Claire's hand. Emma went on. There was nothing else she could do.

As soon as they had passed the wheelhouse, Emma veered toward the rail, hoping to escape the worst of the heat and smoke. Choking, Emma glanced back. Mrs. Gibson was crying again, dragging at Claire's hand, making them both fall behind. Emma waited for them, then pushed them ahead of her and brought up the rear, herding them straight toward the rail.

They were heading toward the dark area she had seen from the saloon's forward door. It was impossible to see anything through the smoke, but if it wasn't on fire yet, they should be able to make it all the way to the bow. Emma kept nudging Mrs. Gibson, trying to hurry her.

Halfway to the rail, Emma stepped over a piece of wood, then saw that it was a man's leg poking out from beneath the boards. Distracted and sickened, she slipped. Her fall was stopped by strong hands on her shoulders. Startled, she twisted around, her heart beating heavily. "Randall . . . ?"

The Yankee was looking down at her. His face was burned; she could see the blisters in the ugly red glow of the fire. "You're smart to try to get up to the bow." When Emma didn't respond, he jerked a thumb toward the stern. "I saw back there. There's so many going over they're pulling each other down."

Emma shrugged, fighting tears, still unable to answer. Her heart was racing. For an instant she had thought Randall had found them, that she could stop pretending to be brave, acting as if she knew what they should do.

Waist-high flames played all along the edge of the abyss now, close to where they had walked only a few minutes before. The saloon was a tunnel of fire, wind shoving the flames through it toward the stern. A few other people were working their way around the wheelhouse toward the rail, dark silhouettes against the orange glare of the fire. There was no time to lose. Emma scowled at the Yankee, then turned to follow Mrs. Gibson and Claire. She hurried to catch up and did not look back.

Emma kept them moving. They traversed the rubble like ants, crawling at times. When they finally reached the explosion-warped railing, they stopped for a few seconds' rest. Emma turned, startled to see the Yankee coming up behind them. He nodded politely again. When she only glared at him, he shrugged. "Are poor manners a family trait?"

Emma blushed, angry. "We don't need Yankee help," she said.

"Well, then, I won't give you any," he answered without hesitation. Just as the Yankee finished his sentence a fan of sparks rose into the air from the crater between the wheelhouses. A second later a vibration shuddered through the main deck beneath their feet.

Wordlessly, Emma grabbed Claire's hand and led her forward. Mrs. Gibson brought up the rear this time. Every time it seemed they could go no farther, Emma managed to find a way through the nightmare maze of wreckage. Every time the smoke cleared a little, she could still see the dark path ahead of them. Behind them, off to their right, the fire was roaring now, driven toward the stern by the steady wind.

"Oh!"

There was so much sadness in Mrs. Gibson's voice that Claire turned, pulling Emma to a stop. Mrs. Gibson was staring down at something, her face blank with shock.

Emma released Claire's hand and turned. "What? What is it?" She held out her right hand. Her hastily made bandage was coming loose. "Come on, please. Mrs. Gibson?"

"We are right . . . right over . . ." Mrs. Gibson pointed, and Emma came closer to follow the gesture. Through a crack in the deck, coal embers sparkled and shone in the darkness below. The explosion had punched them up and out of the long fireboxes and scattered them into the cargo hold below, but some odd trick of the wind had left these coals unfanned. Maybe the collapsing decks had sheltered them. Emma took a quick breath. The dark path might not be dark much longer.

Mrs. Gibson had gone pale beneath the heat flush on her cheeks. Emma could imagine what she was thinking. If the loose boards slid or shifted, a fire could literally erupt from beneath them. Maybe it would whether or not anything moved. The tar on the collapsed hurricane deck could melt and drip onto the coals.

"Please, Mrs. Gibson," Emma said. Mrs. Gibson only looked at her, frozen with fear. Emma pleaded and cajoled, but it was useless.

"We had ought to keep on, Ma'am," the Yankee said quietly from behind them.

Startled, Emma turned. His bony face looked even more angular in the glaring firelight. The hollows around his eyes were deepened into black craters. He raised a hand in greeting, and Emma found herself staring at his fingers. They looked too long, the knuckles too big. Except for his height, he looked like a starved child, fragile and weak.

"We'd best go, Miss," he said, this time aiming his words at Emma. She glowered at him. As if she needed a Yankee to tell her that.

Mrs. Gibson was still, her arms out for balance. She seemed to have forgotten her state of improper dress. She seemed to be unaware of everything but the angry red coals that lay a dozen feet below her. The Yankee came closer. Emma saw him give an involuntary shudder as he leaned to see what Mrs. Gibson was staring at.

"All the more reason to get on across," he said after a few seconds. His voice was steady.

Mrs. Gibson raised her eyes slowly and stared up into his face. He smiled suddenly, then offered her his arm like a man at a dance. "Would you allow me, Ma'am?" Mrs. Gibson's glazed eyes slid down to his hand, then back up to his face. She rested her fingertips lightly on his forearm and nodded as though she had only been waiting for a proper escort.

Emma took Claire's hand and started off. When she glanced back, the Yankee and Mrs. Gibson were walking side by side. They stepped over a board in unison.

Emma hurried along, following the rail. It was broken in places, and she led Claire cautiously past, glancing down at the river. There were hundreds of people thrashing in the water, yelling to companions or to God, begging for help. Many of them clutched pieces of the wreckage, using the shattered lumber as floats. There were men, one atop another, holding fast to the mooring rings and chains that hung from the hull. Emma saw one woman floating upright, her hoop skirt an air-filled buoy.

Finally, they passed the last islands of fire, all still spreading toward the stern. The Yankee and Mrs. Gibson had somehow managed to keep walking side by side. They made their way around the last tangle of unpainted wood, the timbers that had been nailed up to reinforce the hurricane deck against the soldiers' weight. Mrs. Gibson still held the Yankee's arm when they stopped; he was a gentlemanly escort, touching only her elbow, standing very straight.

Emma paused, sucking in deep draughts of fresh air. The smoke was still blowing back, toward the stern. It was a relief to face away from the painful brightness and heat of the fire. Claire sat upon a broken hogshead; the enormous barrel had been blown apart by the explosion. The sugar it had held still stuck to the wood, and Claire pressed some onto her finger, then tasted it.

There was a crowd near the bow, Emma saw, her heart sinking. There were hundreds of people. She put her arm around Claire's shoulders. Claire was shivering. Her dress was damp. So was her hair. Emma looked up and felt fine rain on her face. The stars had winked out. For a moment Emma's heart leaped with hope. If the fire was put out, they could stay on the drifting *Sultana* and wait for some other steamboat to save them— or at least for daylight so they could see which way to swim. She stared at the black sky and tried to see if the clouds were thick or thin, but it was impossibly dark.

The drizzle wet her forehead and cheeks, then stopped as abruptly as it had started. She looked at the Yankee. He had raised his eyes to the sky, too. She wondered if he knew how to swim. Probably not. Even if he did, he might be too weak. Well, he would leave them as soon as he spotted a familiar companion or found a good piece of lumber for a float. There was certainly no advantage to him to stay with two girls and a woman who was so frightened that her eyes were vacant.

"Claire?" Emma waited until Claire was looking at her. "We need something big enough to support us in the water but not too big to carry."

Claire looked puzzled. "But I can swim."

Emma looked out over the dark water, then back at the fire. Claire obviously hadn't understood what was happening in the water: the brutal fights among the men who could not swim, the panicked clutching and desperation. And even if the water were empty, there was no way to know how close or how far the shore was. Swimming in the Mississippi during spring flood wasn't going to be anything like swimming in the pond on their farm. She felt a sudden rush of anger.

Where was Randall? Why hadn't he come back when he was supposed to? It was just like him, running off and getting into some kind of trouble. . . . No, she admitted to herself. It wasn't like him. His temper got him into trouble sometimes, but he usually did what he said he was going to do. He would have come back if he could have. Her anger guttered like a candle in the rain, chilling into fear. Was he hurt somewhere in the muddy streets of Memphis? Had Yankees beat him up again? Or was he here on the *Sultana* somewhere, she thought reluctantly, caught in the explosion?

Emma looked at Mrs. Gibson. She was leaning on the Yankee now. They looked almost silly. A middle-aged woman in a filthy nightgown and a man so thin he appeared to be made of sticks.

Emma looked down. Claire's legs were covered with deep, bloody scratches. Her own feet were cut in so many places it looked like she was wearing dark red slippers. Her hands were raw and full of painful slivers. The sheet-strip bandage on her right hand was stained with blood and tar. Emma shivered. She looked at Claire, then at Mrs. Gibson. The Yankee turned and saw her staring. He met her gaze, then spoke quietly. "We are still alive. Hold to that."

CHAPTER EIGHT

They had to find a float, but here the wooden shards of the wreck were small. The splintered debris nearest the bow was like mounded wooden daggers that slid treacherously beneath Emma's weight. She had left Claire with Mrs. Gibson and the Yankee. They were sitting side by side now. The Yankee looked weak and exhausted. Mrs. Gibson was a little calmer, but Emma could tell she was still terrified.

Prowling the wreckage to find a float, Emma hobbled slowly. Her feet were swelling now, hot and painful. A dead mule lay near the starboard rail. Emma stared at it. Poor animal. It had never known or understood what had happened. The crowd milled around it. Many carried some piece of the wreck, a door or a broken timber. Some were shouting, gesturing emphatically. Others wandered in slow circles or sat, hugging their knees to their chests. All of them kept looking back and forth between the fire and the brown water muscling its way beneath the *Sultana*.

Emma saw Captain Mason. As she watched, he walked first to one man, then another. He took them by the shoulders, looking into their faces. "The wind is containing the fire. The hull is undamaged," she heard him shouting. "Stay aboard . . ."

The rest of his words were drowned out by the mule Emma had thought dead. It squealed and slowly got to its feet, then stood, shaking its head. Suddenly, it seemed to see the fire. It reared, sliding backward and scrambling for footing on the slick deck. It saw the drop, the river below, but by then it could only wrench to one side, unable to stop. It plunged over the bow into the water. Emma caught her breath and moved closer to the rail, trying to see.

The river around the *Sultana* was alive with people and shards of the wreck. The water reflected the fire; those already in the river looked like they were struggling in a cauldron. Near the hull, the mule thrashed and brayed as five or six men grabbed at it and hung on, trying to stay afloat. They can't swim, Emma thought, feeling a cold pressure on her heart. They are going to drown the mule.

Emma looked out across the water. Most of the men were fighting each other, wrestling over a piece of plank, a section of timber or rail. Emma watched, horrified, as one man knocked another from his perch on a stateroom door, then climbed onto it himself, kicking at a third man to keep him away. She fingered the cork belt she wore, her mouth dry.

Abruptly, Emma remembered the mule and looked for it. It was gone. Had they pulled it under so quickly? Had they all drowned? The water was rough and swirling beneath the fire's red glaze. Maybe the mule had just drifted farther from the hull, carried by some current. Maybe. Emma moved back from the rail. She turned and limped back to Claire and Mrs. Gibson. The Yankee was not with them.

"Andrew went to look for a float," Mrs. Gibson informed Emma when she got close enough.

Claire nodded. "He says we are not to talk about drowning."

Emma saw Mrs. Gibson tense. "Maybe we won't have to go in the water at all," she said quickly.

"Best to wait, looks like." The Yankee's voice was just loud enough for Emma to hear. He had come up behind her.

A ruckus near the bow caught Emma's attention. Three or four women were kneeling at the rail, praying. Emma recognized them: the Christian Commission women. A man had stumbled into one of them, nearly knocking her overboard. Now he was shouting at her, his language crude and abusive. The Yankee took a step forward, but just then a burly Negro picked the man up from behind, pinning his arms. He walked him to the edge of the crowd, then set him down carefully not far from where Emma and the others stood watching.

"How dare you touch me?" the man snarled, spinning around. He was wearing a perfect suit of clothes, dark and well fitted, and he spoke in the heavy drawl of the lower Mississippi country. Emma could not remember whether she had ever seen him in the saloon before or not. He was certainly well enough dressed to be a cabin passenger. Emma looked down at her own dress, stained and torn, then at Mrs. Gibson's dirty, soot-smeared nightgown, and smiled wryly.

The well-dressed man stumbled again, and the Negro reached out to steady him. "Don't touch me," the man cried, his voice high with an edge of hysteria. He shoved a hand inside his coat and pulled out a derringer, a shiny little gentleman's gun. A gambler, Emma thought, her heart beating faster as he swung the gun around. Was he crazy? Hadn't there been enough blood and pain already? The gambler took a clumsy step backward, and Emma realized he was drunk. In the same instant the Negro turned, and Emma recognized Hosiah. The gambler leveled the gun, squinting one eye to sight along it.

Emma was stunned. Was he going to shoot Hosiah? She felt a pang inside her chest as though her heart had broken. Hosiah would die for helping a praying woman against a drunken gambler. Nothing made sense anymore. As she watched, Hosiah stood uncertainly, his eyes darting from one side to the other. A small space was opening around them as the crowd noticed the gun. The women praying seemed oblivious. Their eyes were closed; the gambler's shouts were lost in the tangle of voices around them. But the others could hear, and they saw the man's unsteady stance and his shining derringer. They pushed each other, getting back. The gambler elaborately cocked the little pistol, swaying on his feet. Then he leveled it again, less than ten feet from Hosiah's face.

"No," Emma screamed. She thrust Claire at Mrs. Gibson and ran forward, ignoring her painful feet and her thudding heart. She darted through the crowd and leaped at the gambler from behind, pounding her fists against his neck and the back of his head. He lurched and stumbled. Emma fell, sprawling on the deck. The gambler spun around, still holding the gun out at chest level, looking for his attacker. He saw Emma but continued his search, sweeping the gun in a circle.

The instant the gun was no longer pointed at him, Hosiah dodged backward. Cat-quick, the big man timed his movements to the gambler's, staying behind him, out of his sight. At the instant the gambler turned his back on Emma, Hosiah was there, sweeping her up from where she lay. Then he ran.

From a safe distance, both breathing hard, Emma and Hosiah watched the gambler, his face ugly with rage, finish his slow circle. He cursed, lowering the gun. Emma exhaled and her hammering heart eased a little. The gambler staggered, squinting at the men around him.

Pulling Emma lower, Hosiah crouched behind a stack of broken feed sacks. "We mus' hope that no one else upsets him jus' now. If they do, they're dead." Hosiah wiped a hand across his forehead.

Three men carrying a long piece of the deck rail came out of the wreckage and hurried past. Emma watched them. They hesitated at the bow, arguing about whether to jump or wait. Finally, they came away and stood, still talking. Hosiah shook his head. "Too many in the water, all goin' down together." He looked at Emma. "No one's hardly helping no one. 'Cept you."

Emma felt herself blushing. Then shouting drew her attention back to the bow. The three men carrying the railing had apparently decided to jump and had come forward again, one of them shouting orders. Whenever they got close enough, men on every side, wild with fear, grabbed at the rail, trying to wrest it from its original owners. The leader, at his wit's end, ordered the others to force their way. They pushed ahead, knocking several men down. The gambler stumbled in front of them.

"Oh, Lord," Hosiah breathed.

An instant later the gambler was bumped by one of the men—not very hard, but whiskey had altered his balance and he fell, tumbling over the edge, into the water. Emma closed her eyes, knowing she would never forget the expression on his face. He hadn't been angry or drunk as he went over the rail. He had been terrified.

"Emma? Emmmmmaaaa?" Claire's voice pierced both her thoughts and the confusion of voices at the bow. Emma jumped up, wincing.

"Best you go now," Hosiah said evenly. His face was blank. He hadn't stood up, and he didn't even look up at her. "Thank you, Missy. Go on now."

"Good-bye," Emma said, stepping away from Hosiah. He didn't answer her at all this time. When she glanced back at him, he was still sitting in the same position, looking straight ahead.

"I don't want to die," she said to the night, without knowing that she was going to say anything at all. Then she started to cry.

CHAPTER NINE

Emma had stopped crying, not because she felt better, but because her tears had simply dried up. Her mother had always said a person saw more clearly after a good cry, but this time, Emma knew, it wasn't true. Nothing looked different. Certainly nothing looked better.

Facing the bow, their backs to the fire, Claire and Mrs. Gibson sat holding hands. Even with the stiff breeze that kept the flames from coming forward, it was unbearably hot. Claire's cheeks were flushed. Mrs. Gibson's forehead was shiny with sweat. The Yankee had come back from searching unsuccessfully for a float. He'd found a few broken planks and laid them nearby. He sat now, resting, his eyes closed.

The Christian Commission ladies were still praying. Captain Mason continued trying to convince people to stay aboard the *Sultana*. Emma looked around, checking the shadows by the broken feed sacks. Hosiah wasn't there. Maybe he had jumped. She said a prayer for his safety.

Emma looked upstream, wishing for the cabin lanterns of another steamboat. What time was it? The night had already gone on too long, hadn't it? The darkness completely hid the Arkansas shore. The Tennessee side was entirely dark—no city lights. Surely someone at the Memphis docks would see the fire and try to help them. But how long would that be? Two hours? Five?

Emma was hungry and thirsty and tired. Her feet throbbed in time with her pulse. For the first time she thought about her diary, forgotten under the pillow on her bunk. Her mother's leather-bound accounts book. It was ashes now. She felt fresh tears burning behind her eyes. She fingered her waistband. She still had her mother's ring. She would never lose that. Her mother, chin lifted, proud to have a final gift to give her daughter, had given it to her a few days before she had died.

"Missy?"

The voice was so soft that for a moment, Emma wasn't sure that she had heard it.

"Miss?"

She looked up. Hosiah was standing nearby. He wasn't looking at her. He made a tiny motion with his head, a gesture so subtle that if she hadn't been staring at him she would never have noticed it. She told Claire to stay put and walked toward him. He glanced at her as she got close.

"Your poor feet."

She nodded. "I was afraid you had jumped."

Hosiah smiled a little. His face was beaded with sweat. "Not me. Can't swim a lick."

Emma didn't know what to say. She looked back at Claire. She was holding Mrs. Gibson's hand. The Yankee was sitting up again. Mrs. Gibson kept looking at her, disapproval apparent on her face. Randall would think it wasn't proper for her to be talking to Hosiah, either, she knew. She felt a guilty little pang of relief that he wasn't there.

"I foun' what you need," Hosiah said.

Emma turned. "What?"

He smiled. "Well, not ever'thing you need.

But I foun' a float." Emma waited for him to say more, her heart thudding heavily. He arched his brows and looked away from her. "You're standin' on it." Emma looked down at the shattered wood beneath her feet. "Got to look close," Hosiah said.

Emma shook her head. He was either crazy or playing tricks on her. "I don't see anything but wood the size of kindling." She reached down to toss a handful of the debris aside. "This is everywhere. What we need is something big."

Hosiah sighed. "Look closer."

Emma stared at the debris, hands on her hips. Hosiah looked out across the bow, casually swinging one hand back and forth. "See the edge?" He did not look down but kept his eyes moving. He appeared to be scanning the deck.

Emma looked again. This time she noticed a vague rectangular shape buried beneath the debris. Where Hosiah had swept off the broken wood, a jagged piece of the hurricane deck was visible; the planks looked thick, heavy. "I see it," she said, her spirits rising a little. The float was perfect, perhaps eight feet long and two or three feet wide.

"I think we can move it. Me and the Yankee—when the time's right." Hosiah paused, frowning when she didn't react.

Emma hesitated, then spoke her thoughts. "I don't want the Yankee. He just came along."

Hosiah rubbed a hand across his forehead. "I would rather not have the Peachtree woman."

Emma looked up him sharply. "Mrs. Gibson?"

"I was raised 'roun' Baton Rouge," Hosiah said after a long silence. "My mama's still there, a slave 'til she dies maybe now that Lincoln is shot. I hear 'em talkin'." He sighed heavily. "Ever'body 'roun' there knows Peachtree. It ain't a good place for folks." He clasped his hands together and said nothing for a long time.

Emma watched him, not knowing what to say. Did he mean that Mrs. Gibson's family treated their slaves badly? She had seemed to believe the slaves were loyal and loved her family. When Hosiah finally spoke again, he didn't look at her. "Your brother . . . ?" He hesitated, obviously searching for a way to finish the question.

"No," Emma said quickly. "He never came back to our stateroom. He must have got left behind in Memphis."

"Lucky soul. I saw him start the fight with them Yankees. Full of hate, that boy." Hosiah looked out toward the crowd at the bow. They were still jostling and arguing. "Ever'body full of hate."

A high-pitched screeching sound split the air. Emma covered her ears and spun around. Claire was still beside Mrs. Gibson and the Yankee. All three were standing up, looking around wildly. The voices at the bow were silenced. Everyone who had been staring at the water turned back now to face the fire. The rough tearing sound went on, joined by a staccato banging that got louder and louder.

"The wheelhouses," someone yelled. A second later, sparks flew skyward. The enormous shedlike structures that covered the paddle wheels had been undermined by the fire. The one nearest them was collapsing. Planks seemed to leap free as the timbers gave way, a rolling thunder of lumber spilling onto the deck.

Hosiah pulled Emma backward. She stumbled, her bare feet sliding painfully across the wreckage. Hosiah picked her up and carried her toward the bow, stopping short of the crowd to set her down.

"Emma!" Claire was running toward them, her dress flying out behind her. Mrs. Gibson followed, and a little farther behind, the Yankee. Emma felt the already uncomfortable heat of the fire increase as the falling planks of the wheelhouse hit the gutted midsection of the *Sultana*, feeding the flames.

Claire didn't slow until she had wrapped her arms around Emma's waist. Mrs. Gibson hovered close, trying to soothe Claire, touching her back and hair. The Yankee stood a little to one side, facing the fire. The praying women began to sing a hymn. Some of the men joined in; all eyes were wide with fear as they stared at the rising flames.

"The ship's gonna turn now." Hosiah's voice was just loud enough to be heard. Emma saw the Yankee's eyes narrow.

"Turn? Why?"

Emma thought Hosiah was talking nonsense, too. How could the *Sultana* turn? The pilothouse was destroyed. They had been floating aimlessly downriver since the explosion.

"Look." Hosiah pointed at the fire.

Emma followed his gesture. At first she couldn't see anything but the flames, rising higher because of the fresh planks. Then she realized that the flames weren't blowing straight back in the wind anymore. They were slanted slightly toward the wheelhouse that still stood. As she watched, the fire crawled toward it and it began to collapse, the flames leaping to swallow the falling planks.

"He's right. The wheelhouses held us straight against the wind," the Yankee said quietly. He gestured. "With only one, the wind has started us around. It'll switch end for end now."

Hosiah nodded.

Emma watched, her skin prickling, as the flames slanted farther and farther toward the remaining wheelhouse. It sagged, as though drawn by the heat.

"It will surely come this way then. The fire." Mrs. Gibson's voice was barely louder than a whisper, but Emma heard her plainly.

Hosiah and the Yankee exchanged a long look. Emma knew if Randall were here, he would just walk away. He would find a way to save Claire without help from Yankees and Negroes and silly plantation belles. But she wasn't Randall. She was Emma, and she was scared. Did that make her weak enough to tolerate a Yankee—one of the men who had killed her mother, and maybe her father, and destroyed everything she had ever cared about?

Claire pulled at Emma's sleeve, and she looked down. Claire's face was tight with fear. "Are we going to go in the river now?"

Emma shook her head. "I don't think so," she said carefully, aware that the Yankee was watching her sharply. "I am trying to figure what is the best thing to do." The lie was heavy on her tongue, and it left a dirty taste in her mouth. She forced herself to smile. "Come on, Claire," she said as evenly as she could.

Emma gestured at Hosiah, and he stepped away from the others. She tried to make herself say that they would come back in a moment, but she could only manage a false smile as she led Claire along, following after Hosiah. Claire kept looking back, but Emma refused to. She knew that Mrs. Gibson and the Yankee were watching.

Hosiah had stopped near the buried section of deck, but he still looked aimlessly around, watching the fire. It was blowing at an increasingly sharp angle. Soon the wind would be pushing it straight toward them. There were people crawling on the wreckage like ants. Most of them carried pieces of wood already, but they were looking frantically for something bigger, a better bet against the currents and whirlpools of the river.

Emma shivered, soaked with sweat from the fire's heat, but chilled by a sudden gust of wind. The Christian Commission women were gone, except for one who stood on the tip of the bow, her arms spread wide. She was no longer praying but walked back and forth as men jumped from the *Sultana*'s bow, going over in twos and threes like mice escaping a corn bin when the lid is opened. Emma could hear the woman shouting, pleading with those already in the water to stop fighting one another, to behave like men.

"Em, come on," Claire said, pulling at her hand. "We have to go back." She pulled harder.

"No," Emma said, catching Hosiah's eye. "We have to do something first."

She began pushing the ragged chunks of wood and scorched cloth that covered the broken section of deck. She worked her hands under it and lifted. It was heavy. But she could do it. She nodded at Hosiah, and he bent to clear the loose debris from his side.

Emma glanced back at Mrs. Gibson and the Yankee. They were standing close together, facing her. The Yankee looked so weak and thin. Yet he supported Mrs. Gibson as she swayed, one hand fluttering over her nightgown, smoothing it.

"It'd take us all." Hosiah said it quietly. He said no more.

Emma looked at Mrs. Gibson and the Yankee again. She didn't owe either of them anything, did she? Claire liked Mrs. Gibson, but that was just a little girl's attraction to wealth and romantic stories. Randall wouldn't weigh down their chances of survival with a Yankee and a plantation belle. But Randall did a lot of things she wouldn't do.

Emma bent to lift the float. "I can't do it," she said, "I can't leave them."

Hosiah looked at her sharply, then his face softened. "Jus' as well. We might have to explain to Jesus if we lef' somebody, then they drowned."

Emma gestured to the Yankee, shouting. "Can you help us?" He probably couldn't hear what she was saying over the panic and roaring fire, but he had been watching and saw her gesture. He escorted Mrs. Gibson across the rubble.

"Hosiah found this," Emma explained. She looked to Hosiah for confirmation.

He looked at the Yankee. "Got to go straight to the rail. Don' wanna give nobody time to steal it."

The Yankee patted Mrs. Gibson's arm, then gently freed himself. He rubbed a hand over his eyes. "Off to the right as far as we can. It's less crowded."

Hosiah was staring at Mrs. Gibson. She was still close to tears and for a moment, Emma saw what Hosiah must be seeing. Here was a middle-aged woman who had never worked, never had to do any unpleasant task, who had been pampered and cared for all her life by slaves. For the first time in her life she was dirty and scared. Why should Hosiah help her? But then, she thought, why should Hosiah have helped any of them? She was almost certain he could lift the float by himself.

Emma felt fingers of heat slide across her face, touching her dress. She looked up. The flames were coming almost straight toward them, the garish light flickering over their tired soot-streaked faces. There was no time left to worry about who should help whom. She took Claire's hand, then Mrs. Gibson's. She looked to Hosiah. "The three of us will hold hands and jump after you two have gone in with the float. And we should go *now*," she finished, looking from one fire-demon face to the other.

The Yankee nodded, then shook himself like a man trying to awaken from a dream. He stepped in front of her and squatted to get a good hold on the section of deck. Hosiah positioned himself at the other end. Together they lifted it easily. "Hurry now," the Yankee said. Claire and Emma took Mrs. Gibson's hands and followed the two men, half running, half stumbling over the uneven footing. Emma's cut feet ached and stung, but she didn't slow down. The orange flames leaped and snatched at the main deck behind them. The *Sultana* was burning up. The popping and crackling had solidified into a roar.

Ahead of them, screams and wails of fear rose on the bow. Arguments had become hysterical exchanges of shoves and shouts. Even the most timid were being driven over the rail now, and the crowd was dense and frantic, terrified of the heat, the advancing fire.

"Stay close together," the Yankee yelled as they neared a gap in the rail. His face was dripping sweat, and he stared at Emma with intense, narrowed eyes. "You remember she can't swim." He tipped his head toward Mrs. Gibson. Emma nodded. His face *was* a demon's face, bleak, hollow, and distorted. Then he smiled. "There's a clear place," he yelled, looking down and gesturing. "On three," he shouted to Hosiah. Hosiah nodded as the Yankee counted. At the same instant, they jumped sidelong, still holding the float between them. Emma watched the float hit the water, sending a spray in all directions.

Emma tried to step up to the rail, pulling Mrs. Gibson with her. The older woman's terror of the water was obvious. Her hand tightened on Emma's and she balked, turning. Emma felt the brutal heat of the fire on her back. If they hesitated even a minute or two, they would be burned. She released Mrs. Gibson's hand and crossed behind her as though she were reaching for Claire. Instead, without warning, she shoved Mrs. Gibson forward into the water. Then she grabbed Claire and jumped. They were still holding hands when the cold water closed over Emma's head.

CHAPTER TEN

It was dark. Impossibly dark. Something was pulling at Emma's left ankle. She kicked, scraping her right foot down the back of her left leg, trying to dislodge the grip that held her beneath the surface. Mrs. Gibson and Claire were gone. In the endless rush of the water, she could feel her hair streaming across her face, the drag of her dress as it belled out from her body. But her hands were empty. Claire? Where was Claire?

Emma's lungs ached and she kicked again, her fear making her heart pound painfully. The hand that held her down clawed for a better hold, dragging across the cuts on her heel. The sharp stab of pain made Emma double over in the water. Suddenly, the hand loosened and was gone. Desperate to breathe, Emma struggled to swim, but every direction felt the same. Without sunlight to guide her, she was lost in the endless dark water. For a moment, she stopped fighting and let the river carry her.

A few seconds after she stopped fighting, Emma broke the surface and cold air stung her face. She dragged in a long breath, then coughed. Water rushed and swirled against her skin. She took another breath. Then another. The world, the sky, and all her life seemed to be focused on the simple acts of inhaling and exhaling.

"Emma? Emmmaaa . . . Emma!"

Claire's voice brought Emma to her senses. The water around her was the color of reflected flames. Grotesque shapes poked through the orange surface, rising and falling with the currents. The burning hulk of the *Sultana* was close, too close. Emma stared up at it. It towered above her, the flames leaping at the sky.

"Emmmaaaa!"

Emma began to swim toward Claire's voice. There were others in the water around her, but she swam quietly and avoided them, watching carefully, afraid every time someone came close. Finally, she saw the float and swam a straight line, coming up behind Claire to grab the edge. Claire wrenched around and smiled giddily at her, her eyes rimmed in white, her skin pale. "I'm all right," Emma reassured her sister, trying not to let her fear into her voice.

"Thank the Lord," Hosiah said. His voice was full of gratitude. He was still hanging on to the end of the float he had carried. His shoulders were hunched, his forearms on the planks. The stiffness in his posture belied his fear of the water.

"We are so relieved," Mrs. Gibson said from her place almost directly across from Emma. Beside her, the Yankee held on grimly, water streaming from his hair. He nodded without speaking; he looked near the end of his strength. Mrs. Gibson followed Emma's glance. "Andrew tried to find you. He dove under so many times we feared for him." She had half turned when the float bobbled with the current. She lost her hold with one hand and took in a mouthful of water. The Yankee held her steady while she coughed and regained her grip on the planks.

Emma moved hand over hand until she was close to Claire. "I want Randall," Claire whispered.

"I know," Emma told her. "I do, too." The cold water swirled around Emma's legs and stung the cuts on her feet.

"I am so hungry," Hosiah said. "Biscuits would be jus' perfect."

Andrew smiled a little. "In Cahaba prison, we had two rules. We didn't talk about dying. Or food."

"Food?" Claire echoed. "Because you were so hungry?"

The Yankee cleared his throat, and Emma saw him straighten, visibly trying to rouse himself. "We lived on ground-up corn husks and rancid salt pork jest full of maggots. I had friends get gangrene from little scratches, it was that filthy. We used to . . ." His voice dropped until it was hard to hear. He cleared his throat like he meant to go on, but then he didn't.

Hosiah shook his head. "I heard 'em talkin', tellin' their stories. I don' know how you all lived."

The Yankee smiled again, a skull-grin on his haggard, weary face. "We got a dirty old blanket once, my partner and I. Tricked a guard out of it—a filthy blanket you wouldn't give to a dog. Lord, we were happy as kids with a sack of candy."

Emma tried to think of something to say, but she couldn't. No one said anything for a long time. Finally Andrew cleared his throat again. "Hate is an awful way to stay alive."

"Amen," Hosiah agreed, glancing at Mrs. Gibson.

The float suddenly dipped, following the contour of the water. It spun and rode the current crosswise for a while. Claire screamed when it dropped a second time.

"It's jus' the shape of the river," Hosiah shouted at her. "There's a bar or a ridge down there. Jus' hang on tight."

"We have to get away from the *Sultana*," the Yankee said. His voice was faint. He pointed.

Emma followed his gesture, looking upstream for the first time since she caught hold of the float. She gasped. The *Sultana* was chasing them down the river. It loomed above them like a firestorm.

"Kick," Emma told Hosiah. She and Claire showed him how. Mrs. Gibson used one arm to paddle, and the Yankee drew his rope belt through a crack in the float and swam, pulling the float. Together, they moved across the current.

Finally, the *Sultana* was no longer behind them; it rode the current beside them across a widening gap. Emma could see a few men still huddled on the very front of the bow, bent over, nearly overcome with the heat. Many more were still clinging for their lives to the chains and tackle hanging from the hull.

Hosiah, kicking his feet as Emma had showed him, kept pushing the float along steadily. The Yankee rested off and on, as did Emma. Claire and Mrs. Gibson tired more quickly. By the time they were riding the broad back of the river parallel to the wreck, far enough away to be safe from burning wreckage, both had long since gone silent, using all their remaining strength just to hold on. The float rose and fell, dipping low on one side, then the other. Emma moved closer to Claire, ready to help if she lost her hold. Once the float leveled out, she saw that the Yankee had moved closer to Mrs. Gibson.

For a long time, they did not speak. The water was cold, but the air was even colder. Emma lowered herself into the river so that only her neck and face were exposed. She flexed her hands over and over again, trying to keep the numbing cold at bay. She kept looking across the float at the dark shape of the Yankee. He had dived for her. Why? He was so weak. Mrs. Gibson was praying again, her voice underlying the sounds of the river.

"Where's the alligator?" Emma asked suddenly, looking at Hosiah.

"Somebody killed it, Missy," Hosiah said. "Jus' stabbed it through and took the crate for a boat."

"I wanted the alligator to go free," Claire said softly.

Hosiah heard her. "Back to his ol' swamp."

The float tilted high on Emma's side, then fell. "Sandbars clear 'long this stretch," Hosiah said. "Flood pushes 'em up."

As if to confirm his words, the float began to rise and fall, gently at first, then slamming against the water. Claire cried out. Emma could do nothing but hang on and wait for the battering to stop. When it finally did, Claire was holding the edge of the float with one hand and Emma's sleeve with the other. Mrs. Gibson and the Yankee were close together; she was still praying with her eyes closed.

"Halloo!"

The shout took Emma off guard. The voices had been dimming behind them. This one was very close. Whoever it was tried to shout again, but a fit of choking stopped him. It went on so long that Emma began to fear it would never stop.

"Hallooo?" the call finally came again.

"Here," Claire called. "This way."

"Where?" the voice cracked. The man was upstream and not far away.

"Friend," the Yankee called out, before Claire could answer again. "We can take one or maybe two. More than that will sink us."

"I am alone," the voice came back. Something about the heavy cotton-country accent was familiar, but Emma could not place it. She shivered, waiting. A few seconds later a form separated itself from the rushing blur of dark water. It was instantly apparent that the man didn't know how to swim, that he was supported by a few broken boards clasped against his chest. He flailed madly with his free arm, and they could hear him gagging on river water. It took him a long time to maneuver close enough to reach out and grab on next to Hosiah. He tried to hoist his planks onto the float but he fumbled at the edge, losing first one plank, then two more to the dark water.

"Damnation," the man exploded, watching them disappear. As he turned back, his face was dimly lit by the *Sultana*'s distant fire. It was the drunken gambler. Emma heard Claire catch her breath and knew that she had recognized him, too. Had Hosiah? She couldn't tell. He had moved over a little, giving the newcomer room.

The man wiped water off his face and hitched himself higher on the float. He looked at them one by one, finishing with Hosiah. "Well, well. Two girls, a fat woman, a starved Yankee, and a darkie." If he was still drunk, his speech showed no signs of it. Probably, Emma thought, the cold water had sobered him. Claire moved closer to Emma. Hosiah moved a little farther from the man.

"There is no need for that kind of talk," the Yankee said.

The gambler laughed. "You are hardly in a position to enforce that, sir."

"Or maybe I am," the Yankee said. "Can you swim, mister?"

The gambler hesitated, then laughed again. Before he could answer, the float swooped down a trough in the current. He lost his grip, then regained it, cursing aloud. They hit calmer water and the float leveled.

The gambler was silent, his face turned away from them, looking out into the darkness. Hosiah had slumped forward, his forearms on the boards. He raised his head. "Lord, that scares me."

Before anyone could say anything more the river began to lift and drop the float again. Cold water slithered over the float, fanning into spray when it dipped, running off when it rose again. Emma hung on, spitting out muddy water, trying to encourage Claire while her own heart pounded in fear. Her hands were clumsy with cold. It was harder and harder to hang on.

When they finally got to a smooth stretch of water, Claire was sobbing with fear. The Yankee was silent, as was Hosiah. Mrs. Gibson stopped her prayers for a moment. "I cannot hold on much longer."

"Nor I," the Yankee said very quietly.

"Let go now, then," the gambler said. "Be a noble Yankee and save these children. Lighten the float. Or perhaps the darkie should go first. He still deserves a lesson, I do believe."

Without any further warning, the gambler swung a fist at Hosiah's face. It connected with a sodden thud that made Emma cry out. Hosiah slumped and the gambler hit him again. Hosiah slid a little lower, turning his head.

Mrs. Gibson screamed and the Yankee yelled something, but Emma couldn't understand either one of them. All she could see was good-hearted Hosiah trying to keep his grip on the float as the gambler battered his face. The current carried them down an incline ending in a trough so narrow that the float tipped steeply, then flattened again, slapping the surface of the water. The gambler stopped his assault to hang on.

Hosiah's face was cut. Emma could see the red of the blood that coursed down his cheek and chin. For a moment, the fact that she could see so clearly seemed more important than anything else in her cold-dulled mind. It was almost morning, she thought. Morning. The night had finally ended.

The gambler hit Hosiah once more. Hosiah took the blow without a sound. He clutched at the edge of the float, more afraid of the water than the gambler. Emma couldn't stand it. She moved around Claire, closer to the gambler.

"Emma, no." It was the Yankee. She glanced at him. There was another awful thud as the gambler's fist connected with Hosiah's cheekbone.

"Hit him back," the Yankee shouted. "Hit him! You're twice his strength. God, I wish I could—"

"Shut your mouth, Yankee," the gambler spat. "You don't know anything about this."

"Fight back," Emma pleaded, her voice low. Hosiah shook his head. Whether he was refusing their advice or just trying to clear his thoughts, Emma couldn't tell. The gambler raised his fist again, before Hosiah could react. "Hang on tight," Emma whispered to Claire. Then she sank beneath the surface, one hand trailing along the edge of the float. When she felt the corner, she came up, shaking her hair back out of her eyes.

The gambler was still turned away from her, his right fist in the air again. His left hand gripped the edge of the float. Emma clenched her hand and hit him across the knuckles as hard as she could. Startled, the gambler whirled, cursing, losing his grip, then regaining it. He grabbed the collar of Emma's dress and swung her around, shoving her away from the float, into the current. She struggled to make her weary arms and legs move, to keep her face clear of the water.

"Emma!" Claire was screaming. "Emma!"

Emma saw the gambler raise his hand once more; then she could only fight the water, trying to swim. The current was overpowering. She tried to stay calm as the river spun her around. Her ears were full of cold water, and her hair streamed across her face. She swallowed a mouthful of the muddy water and began to choke. The river was too big. There was an eternity of water.

Emma's arms felt like wood, dead and heavy. She couldn't see the float, couldn't hear anyone's voice. She was alone with the river now, and it was much, much stronger than she was. She sank a little, then struggled to the surface. Rough water buffeted her and she sank again. When she felt the hand on her shoulder, she was almost certain it wasn't real. But then she heard the Yankee's voice.

"You have to help me."

She turned in the water to see his haggard face. She felt him trying to pull her through the water. She began to kick her legs sideways like a scissors opening and closing, trying to time her strokes with his. After a while he no longer held her dress—she clutched at his shirt. They fought the water together.

After a long time, Emma heard Mrs. Gibson and Claire calling out to them. She tried to kick harder and couldn't, but she refused to stop. At last, they were alongside the float, and the Yankee placed her hands on the wood. Emma sagged, feeling Claire's little hands on her face and back.

"Emma! Emma?"

"I'm . . . all right," Emma managed, then opened her eyes.

The Yankee was slowly working his way back around to take his place by Mrs. Gibson. She was sobbing and he could only look at her, too exhausted to say any words of comfort.

Emma looked past Claire to see the gambler staring at her. "Well, well. A noble Yankee after all."

"Stop. Be still now." It was Hosiah. He had raised himself up; his face was dark with blood. The gambler lifted his hand, but this time Hosiah did not look away, did not cringe.

The gambler stared as Hosiah shifted his grip, moving toward him. But then, suddenly, Hosiah wrenched at the float, ripping one plank off, using his right fist like a hammer to bang it free from beneath. The float jittered and rocked. Hosiah pulled a second, then a third plank free. His strength was obvious, incredible. So was his rage. The nails squealed, torn out of the wood.

"What are you doing?" the gambler demanded. "Are you crazy? You'll drown us all."

Hosiah held up the planks in one hand. His voice was level. "Take these. Leave us." He laid the planks where the gambler could reach them.

The gambler hesitated. Hosiah's face was terrifying. His eyes, narrowed to slits, were shining through the blood. Emma glanced at the Yankee. His eyes were open now, fixed upon the gambler. Mrs. Gibson and Claire were staring, too, their faces bleak and angry.

Without speaking, the gambler grabbed at

the planks. He held them tightly to his chest and splashed into the water. Once he was gone, the Yankee smiled weakly, his hair dripping water. He looked like a skeleton, his skin the color of bleached bone. Claire was crying quietly. Her eyes closed again, Mrs. Gibson prayed in a whisper.

Emma drew in a long breath. "Thank you," she said. "Thank you, Andrew." The Yankee nodded, letting her know he had heard her. The sun bulged above the horizon, sending gold across the muddy water.

CHAPTER ELEVEN

Emma saw it first. She blinked. Then she shouted. Her voice was rough with cold and exhaustion. Hosiah roused himself enough to open his eyes. "A boat!" Emma slapped at the water in almost hysterical jubilation. "A boat!"

Hosiah smiled a little and tried to hail the launch.

Mrs. Gibson and Claire added their feeble voices to the raspy chorus. One of the men in the launch turned, then pointed, alerting his companions. They began rowing, yelling encouragement as they came across the brown water. Emma closed her eyes. They were saved.

The men pulled Claire from the water first and wrapped her in a blanket. Emma was next, then Mrs. Gibson. Andrew was nearly unconscious as they brought him up. Once out of the water, Hosiah began to shake so violently that his whole body trembled. On the way back to the levee, he sat in the bow and held Andrew across his lap like a child, chafing Andrew's hands and feet and talking to him quietly. Mrs. Gibson huddled with Claire and Emma, shivering and praying. Emma watched the shoreline get closer, scanning the faces. Where was Randall? Was he there?

Memphis was noisy. Buckets of pitch and tar had been lit as torches and they still burned, their oily smoke blowing out over the water. Unconscious survivors and the bodies of people who had drowned lined the wharf. Crowds milled in the streets—people had thronged to the riverside to watch the survivors as they were brought to shore. Ambulances and omnibuses were backed up to the cobbled levee. Stamping their hooves impatiently, horses breathed steam into the morning chill.

As soon as Emma and the others stepped across the plank to the levee, the launch that had brought them cast off again to renew its search for *Sultana* passengers. Hosiah carried Andrew. Mrs. Gibson had wrapped a blanket around her shoulders like a cape. She held the edges together over her nightgown. Claire, her teeth chattering, was still shuddering with cold.

"Let us take that one to Overton Hospital," a man directed, bustling past Emma. "He needs a doctor." Reluctantly, Hosiah relinquished Andrew to the ambulance drivers. Emma watched as they loaded Andrew with five or six others, then whipped the horses into a gallop and disappeared up the street. Overton Hospital. Where was that?

Emma tried to wrap her blanket tighter, but her hands were numb, clumsy. All around them, people were approaching the survivors, offering help, money, clothing. Emma kept watching for Randall, but he did not come.

After a time, a woman came toward them from the crowd and approached Claire. She knelt before her, her lovely dress trailing in the mud. She smiled up into Claire's face. "Are you all right, dear?" Claire nodded. "Is this your mother?" The woman indicated Mrs. Gibson, who was blinking in the early sunlight, standing uncertainly, her hair a sodden mass of tangles down her back. Claire shook her head.

"She's our friend," Emma said quickly.

The woman nodded. "You can all three come

to my home. We brought the carriage to see how we could help." She pointed back toward the crowd, and Emma saw a dark-haired man looking at them expectantly.

"You go on, Missy," Hosiah said. His eyes were dull and his voice sounded far away.

Claire took Hosiah's hand. "Come with us."

The woman cleared her throat. "Well, no. I don't have a way to care for him."

"He can come with us," a voice broke in. A tall Negro stood nearby, his hair white with age. "Son?" He took Hosiah's arm.

Hosiah smiled a little. "I'd be obliged."

Emma hesitated. She watched Hosiah walk away. He had almost turned the corner when she found her voice. "Hosiah?" He looked back. "Tomorrow. Come here early. We have to find Randall and Andrew."

Hosiah nodded, exaggerating the gesture so she'd see it. He waved and went on, walking slowly, heavily. Emma took Claire's hand, then Mrs. Gibson's. They followed the woman to a carriage and got in. The horses' hooves clattered on the cobblestone. Emma heard everyday shouts and greetings as they rounded a corner. Sunlight drenched the streets. The buildings looked solid, perfect. It was Thursday morning and Memphis was waking up.

April 28, 1865
Memphis, Tennessee

Mrs. Lyrett has brought me a journal. It will
never replace mother's account book, but I am
grateful for it and for all of her help. There is
so much in my heart to write. I don't know
where to begin. Randall is alive and well. He
was in one of the launches, helping to pull
people from the river. He feels terrible about
missing the Sultana when she left Memphis—
he was lost in the streets and late returning.
He cried when we told him the story of the
long night. We are so very lucky. So many
died. Many more were horribly hurt, burned.
It is awful how many families will never see
their returning soldiers. I pray every day for
Father.

Mrs. Gibson is recovering, though she's still
in bed. Mrs. Lyrett gives her soup and talks
with her endlessly. Claire is much better, has
eaten meal after meal from Mrs. Lyrett's
kitchen. Randall wired Uncle Simeon but got
no answer. Still, in a few days we will board
another paddle wheeler and finish our journey.
Mrs. Gibson will travel with us. She offered
us a place in her home until we can find
Uncle Simeon or arrange something on our

own. She says Claire and I can go to school.

The saddest time of all was this morning when Hosiah and I walked to Overton Hospital. It was a long way, and we were both very tired upon getting there. Then the terrible news. Andrew has died. He was too weak to stand the cold in the water, the doctor said. I cried and I am ashamed that I hated him so. He used up the last bit of his own strength to save me. Mrs. Gibson cried for hours. She says she will find out if he has a family. If he does, Randall has agreed we will send them one of our last two gold coins and a letter telling them how bravely Andrew died. I will always remember him and wish that I could have bid him farewell. He was a friend.

Hosiah says he will stay here in Memphis with the family who helped him at the dock. They have a farrier's and blacksmith's shop and can use his help. Hosiah says his new friends know someone who can write a little and that he will send us a letter at Mrs. Gibson's house. I have promised to answer. And so, I suppose we all go on from here, except Andrew. We are alive. We will be all right. I am holding to that.